"Garth said something about how God doesn't judge the way people do. God looks at the heart."

Link touched Annie's cheek lightly, wanting to find a way to erase her doubts. "Anyone who looks at your heart sees how much you love that little girl. Don't ever doubt that."

Her cheek moved against his fingers as she smiled. He felt the tension begin to drain out of her.

"Then I guess we'd better pray that the social worker looks with God's eyes. And that God doesn't care that I burned a quiche."

The attempt at humor relieved him, and he realized he'd been holding his breath. One part of his mind looked at himself, amazed. When had he ever worked so hard just to ease someone else's hurt?

This wasn't just someone else, he thought. This was Annie.

Books by Marta Perry

Love Inspired

A Father's Promise #41
Since You've Been Gone #75
Desperately Seeking Daddy #91
The Doctor Next Door #104
Father Most Blessed #128
A Father's Place #153
Hunter's Bride #172
A Mother's Wish #185
A Time To Forgive #193
Promise Forever #209
Always in Her Heart #220

*Hometown Heroes

MARTA PERRY

has written everything from Sunday school curriculums to travel articles to magazine stories in twenty years of writing, but she feels she's found her writing home in the stories she writes for Love Inspired.

Marta lives in rural Pennsylvania, but she and her husband spend part of each year at their second home in South Carolina. When she's not writing, she's probably visiting her children and her beautiful grandchildren, traveling or relaxing with a good book. She loves hearing from readers and will be glad to send a signed bookplate on request. She can be reached c/o Steeple Hill Books, 233 Broadway, New York, NY 10279, or visit her on the Web at www.martaperry.com.

ALWAYS IN HER HEART

MARTA PERRY

Love Inspired®

Published by Steeple Hill Books™

STEEPLE HILL BOOKS

Steeple
Hill®

ISBN 0-373-87227-5

ALWAYS IN HER HEART

Visit us at www.steeplehill.com

Printed in U.S.A.

Man looks on the outward appearance,
but the Lord looks at the heart.
—*1 Samuel* 16:7

This story is dedicated with great affection to Carol and Bill. Old friends are the best. And, as always, to Brian.

Chapter One

"Marry you?" Annie Gideon stared, incredulous, at Link Morgan's determined face. "Why would I marry you? I don't even like you."

The annoyed expression Link so often wore when he looked at her intensified. "Maybe you'd better figure out a way, Annie. Because if you don't, we're both going to lose what we value most."

The headache that had been throbbing since the double funeral the day before clutched at her temples. "Why on earth are you saying something so preposterous now? And why here?"

Link gave a quick glance around the living room of her sister's house, as if reminding himself that the delicate French Provincial furniture was as charming as Becca had been. Then he zeroed in on Annie.

Her heart gave a rebellious thump. Everything about Link, from his piercing dark eyes to his square jaw to his confident stride, proclaimed that here was a man who knew what he wanted and would do whatever it took to get it. She, of all people, knew just how accurate that impression was.

He'd exchanged the dark suit he'd worn at the funeral for gray pants and a black sweater that still gave an aura of mourning. But mourning or not, he was clearly back to business.

"Sorry. I know this is a bad time." His deep voice softened slightly. "But time is just what we don't have. The fact that Davis and Becca died without making a will has put both of us between a rock and a hard place."

The pastel room swam before her eyes, and the scent of the lilies she'd brought from the funeral cloyed. She forced back a wave of sorrow. If she didn't control it, grief for her sister would submerge every other instinct. She'd be no good to anyone, especially Marcy.

The thought of her twenty-month-old niece, napping unaware in the upstairs nursery, strengthened her. She frowned at the man who'd been Davis's partner and best friend.

"I don't see what's so complicated about it. Doesn't Marcy automatically inherit everything?"

"Exactly." Link's straight, even features might have been chiseled from stone. "That's the problem. The baby inherits this house, whatever property Davis owned and Davis's thirty percent of the firm."

Light dawned. He was worried about the construction company he and Davis had shared.

"I can't imagine that will make any difference to the way you run the company. Marcy's certainly not going to interfere."

Contempt probably sounded in her voice. Link's best friend and her sister were dead, victims of a wet road and a missing guardrail, and apparently all Link could think about was his business.

"You don't get it, do you." A strand of dark hair fell on his forehead, accentuating his lowered brows. "What do you imagine is going to happen now to all this?" His gesture seemed to take in the gracious house that had been in the Conrad family for generations, the construction company, even the sleeping child upstairs.

She turned away from that intimidating stare, trying to get her bearings in a world that was suddenly alien. The wide front windows of Becca's home overlooked the town square with its flower beds and gazebo, surrounded by early-twentieth-century shops. She caught a glimpse of blue lake through the trees. Lakeview was a delightful Finger Lakes village, but it had been her sister's place. She didn't belong here.

"I don't know about the property," she said finally. "I guess Davis's lawyer will have to figure that out. If I have to stay until things are settled, I will. Then I'll take Marcy back to Boston with me."

"They won't let you."

For an instant her mind refused to process the

words. Then she spun to face him, the room seeming to spin with her. "What are you talking about? Who won't let me?"

"Little Marcy inherits everything." He spaced the words out as if he spoke to someone who didn't have a grasp of the English language. "Whoever controls her controls her inheritance. If you think Davis's cousins will let you walk away with Conrad property, you'd better think again. Frank and Julia are the only Conrad relatives left, except for an elderly uncle."

She told herself he was crazy, because she couldn't face the possibility that he was right. "Frank and Julia Lester don't want to be bothered with a baby. Even though they lived nearby, the Lesters have never shown any interest in Marcy." In fact, Becca had said the Lesters bluntly proclaimed they wouldn't have a family because children might interfere with their social life.

"Maybe not." A bitter smile touched Link's mouth and then vanished. "But now that Marcy's inherited, I suspect the Lesters are going to discover that they've always adored her and want her to live with them."

She pressed her hand hard against the oval marble-topped table. "They can't have her. They don't love her. I'm Marcy's closest living relative. With Davis's parents deceased and my mother's illness, there isn't anyone else. Naturally I'll take responsibility for her."

"Naturally." Something that might have been amusement threaded Link's deep voice. "Annie is the responsible one. You always took care of Becca, didn't you?"

"I always tried." Memory pricked her. "Just as you always tried to protect Davis, even when he didn't need protecting."

A grimace marred Link's features. "I wondered how long it would take you to bring that up. It's been eight years, Annie. Can't you forget?"

"No." She shot the word back before she considered, but it was true. She could never forget the summer she and Becca had met Davis and Link, because that was when she'd tumbled head-over-heels into first love.

He seemed to consider that abrupt negative for a moment. "Why? Davis and Becca forgave me. Why can't you?"

"I have forgiven you." Forgiveness for a wrong done to her was easy. Forgiveness for a wrong done to the little sister she'd always protected wasn't. Still, she tried to live each day as a Christian, and that mandated forgiveness.

"You can forgive." His voice went soft. "But you can't forget."

When Link's bass voice went down to that low rumble, it had a deleterious effect on her morale. She shook her head, trying to shake off the feeling.

"None of that matters now. What's important is Marcy. Becca would expect me to take care of the baby if something happened to her." Pain clutched her heart at the words. None of them had anticipated the accident.

"I don't suppose you have that in writing."

"No."

"I didn't think so." Link rubbed the back of his neck as if he had a headache, too. "That's what makes it so chancy. You might believe Becca wanted you to take care of Marcy, and I might believe Davis would want me to run the company for his daughter, but neither of us can prove it. That makes us vulnerable."

"To the Lesters, I suppose." She still couldn't believe that. "Frank has been around helping with the arrangements. He hasn't given a hint he's thinking any such thing."

"You don't know Frank as well as I do—"

Link caught her hand in a quick, impatient movement. The warmth of his fingers startled her. She hadn't known how cold she was until he touched her.

"He smiles and smiles, but all the while he's looking for a weakness."

She pulled her hand away. She didn't know about Frank, but showing any weakness to Link could only be bad for her.

"Why did you let Frank buy into the company, if you feel that way about him?"

"We needed some investors a couple of years ago in order to get a loan for the lakeside project." He shot her a questioning look. "You know about the project, don't you?"

"Not much. Just that you and Davis are building homes along the east side of the lake." Becca had mentioned the project briefly, but she'd been much more engrossed in Marcy's new tooth than in business.

"The project is a gamble for a company the size of Conrad and Morgan, so Davis thought we should form a limited corporation. Frank wanted in, and Davis wouldn't turn down his cousin. Now Frank wants all of it."

"You can't know that."

"I know." His mouth set grimly, sending a little tremor down her spine. "I've given this a lot of thought, Annie. You're Marcy's closest relative, but you're an unmarried career woman. I was Davis's best friend and partner, but I'm not a blood relative. Separately, our claim to Marcy is weak, but if we were married—"

"We can't get married just like that." She rushed the words, needing to deny that this thing could possibly be real. The thought of losing Marcy sent a chill to her very soul.

Please, Father. This can't be happening, can it?

"We're not talking about romance here, Annie. I'm telling you, marriage is the only way." He glanced at his watch. "We can apply for a license today and—"

"No!" She folded her arms tightly, hoping her voice projected strength and conviction. "I won't let you rush me into something like this. First, I don't believe you're right about the Lesters. Julia's always made it clear she doesn't want a child. And second, even if you are, I won't jump into marriage until I've explored every other option.''

"All the details in a row, in other words.'' He clipped off the words as if he disliked them, his eyes narrowing. "You really are the perfect accountant, aren't you.''

"There's nothing wrong with paying attention to detail.''

"There is if it keeps you from getting what you want.''

"I suppose you think it's better to charge right at what you want, no matter who gets hurt.'' Maybe that defined the difference between them. The past blurred into the present. "I won't do things that way, not when Marcy's future is at stake.''

"Fine.'' Link swung away from her, exasperation in every line of his tall, strong figure. "You think, and figure, and debate.'' He tossed the words over his shoulder at her. "If you end up by losing Marcy, maybe you'll remember I gave you fair warning.''

He stalked out of the room, and she heard the front door slam behind him.

Annie sank into the nearest chair, fists clenching on its brocade arms. She'd certainly come out of that encounter the worse for wear. Link's quick mental leaps had always outrun her need to unravel any knotty problem step by careful step.

She closed her eyes, shutting out Becca's pastel living room. Eight years ago, she and Becca had been college students, and Becca had talked her into working at the shore instead of taking the internship she'd been offered.

"You don't want to spend the summer in a stuffy old bank." Becca's face had lit with anticipation. "We'll find great jobs at the beach. Think of the gorgeous guys we'll meet."

Becca always had managed to meet gorgeous guys everywhere, and they both knew their parents wouldn't allow Becca to go unless Annie went to take care of her. But she'd said yes, because she couldn't bear to see Becca's disappointment if she hadn't.

The jobs hadn't been wonderful, but they had met Davis and Link, college roommates who'd had the same idea as Becca. Davis, fair and smiling, had taken one look at Becca and been a goner. His tall, dark-haired friend hadn't had Davis's looks and polish, but he'd made Annie's heart do something she'd never felt it do before. She'd always been careful, never falling in and out of love the way Becca did. Then Link reached right past her guard and touched her heart.

Everything had been perfect—until Link decided his friend was getting too serious about Becca. In an instant he'd turned into someone Annie didn't know—grim, determined, implacable. If he'd bothered to explain what he had against Becca—

Well, no. Link couldn't have come up with any

reason that would have satisfied her for trying to part Becca and Davis. She and Link had quarreled, if you could call it quarreling when one person argued and the other stood as unmoving as a…a block of granite.

Davis and Becca had married in spite of everything Link had done to stop it. The two men had eventually mended the rift, settling in Davis's hometown to start their construction business. Becca had even asked Link to be Marcy's godfather.

Everyone had been able to forget the quarrel but her. She'd seen Link every time she came to visit Becca, but she'd maintained a polite, smiling distance. The man had dented her heart and hurt her beloved sister. She wasn't about to become his dearest friend.

But now he didn't want her to be his friend. He wanted her to be his bride.

A chill went through her in spite of the warm September sunshine that poured through the windows. If Link was right about the Lesters…

Please, show me what to do, Lord. Every time I think of Link's words, I feel paralyzed.

She badly needed some impartial advice. She reached for the white phone on the marble-topped table. But who?

Her father was probably exhausted from the drive back to Boston and the effort of soothing her mother's distress at his absence. Alzheimer's had robbed her mother of knowing who he was, but she did seem to realize she depended upon him.

Dad would have to know, but not yet. She dialed Sam Watson's number.

Sam, an attorney she'd dated casually over a year ago, had remained a friend even after they'd drifted apart. That seemed to be the romantic pattern of her life. Maybe the ability to inspire passion had just been left out of her makeup. If so, she was doing very nicely without it, especially after the fiasco with Link.

Once Sam answered, she quickly described the situation, leaving out Link's proposal. She waited for Sam to say something reassuring.

"I'm not an expert in family law." Sam's tone was cautious. "Your sister and her husband ought to have spelled out their wishes in a will. You need a good local attorney."

For once she was impatient with caution. "Give me your best guess. Will I have problems getting custody of Marcy?"

"Custody wouldn't be a sure thing, even if your sister had named you in her will. The court could still exercise its discretion." He hesitated. "If these cousins do file for custody, the court might favor a local married couple over an out-of-state, single, working woman."

That was what Link had said, and her heart sank. "What can I do? I might feel differently if they even cared about Marcy, but they don't."

"Get a good attorney," he said. "And pray for a sympathetic judge."

She sat staring at the phone after she'd hung up,

trying to think her way through this. Had Becca ever mentioned an attorney she might call?

She was leafing through Becca's address book when she heard a faint wail. Dropping the book, she hurried up the stairs to Marcy's room.

Becca had decorated the nursery with pastel-colored animal figures. A line of yellow giraffes ambled across the wallpaper border, while a pink elephant formed the base of a lamp. Marcy stood in the white canopied crib, shaking the railing impatiently. Her fine blond hair curled damply around her face, and her cheeks were rosy with sleep.

"Up, up," she demanded, holding out chubby arms to Annie. "Up, Nan."

She'd happily be called "Nan" until Marcy mastered "Aunt Annie." She scooped her niece from the crib, putting her cheek against the soft curls. "Did you have a good sleep, sweetpea?"

Marcy patted her face, and Annie's heart melted. Nothing had prepared her for the wave of sheer love she'd felt when she first held her sister's child. *Blood of my blood,* she'd thought, and known the infant had her heart in a tiny hand.

She dressed Marcy, listening to her mostly incomprehensible chatter, and took her downstairs. The doorbell rang as they reached the family room. Her defenses went up instantly, and she marched to the front door carrying Marcy. If Link had come back to press her for a decision again—

But it wasn't Link. Frank and Julia Lester stood at the door, wearing identical smiles.

"Frank. Julia. I wasn't expecting you." She had an irrational urge to close the door in their faces. She stepped back. "Please, come in."

"Naturally we came by to see how you're doing." Frank led the way into the living room as if this were his home. "Yesterday was so difficult for all of us."

"So difficult," Julia echoed, her expression blank.

"Thank you." They all stood awkwardly on the pale beige carpeting Becca had chosen. She should ask them to sit down, but if they stayed, she might blurt out Link's suspicions. "I appreciate everything you did to help, you know."

"As Davis's closest relative, I felt responsible. Who else would do it?" Frank looked at his wife as if silently prompting her.

Julia glanced down at her silk jacket, then held out her hands to Marcy. "Why don't you let me take her."

Annie's arms tightened around the baby, tension traveling along her nerves. Frank smiled, and Link's words echoed.

Frank smiles and smiles, and all the time he's looking for a weakness.

She told herself she didn't believe that, but Link's suspicions affected her anyway. "She just woke up. She doesn't feel like going to someone else just now."

Julia stepped closer, determination in every line of

her fashionably thin figure. "The baby loves Cousin Julia. She'll come to me."

Ridiculous, to feel menaced by the woman. Annie tried to produce a smile. "Not now. Much as I'd like to chat with you, I have a great deal to do. So if you'll excuse me…"

"Of course, of course. I'm sure you're busy getting packed to go back to Boston." Frank's smile didn't falter. He moved closer, almost as if he and Julia were closing in on her.

Annie's tension jacked upward. "I'm not—"

"We realize how eager a career woman like you must be to get back to your job." Frank reached for Marcy. "So we've come for the baby."

He should have known Annie wouldn't let herself be swept along with his idea. Link swiveled his desk chair to look out the window of Conrad and Morgan, Builders. Their tiny offices were located diagonally across the town square from the house that had been "the Conrad place" for generations.

No, he should have approached Annie in a way she'd understand. She'd always had to have every detail at her fingertips.

That had come between them before, when he couldn't explain why he was so opposed to Davis's abrupt decision to propose to Becca, bound as he'd been by promises and obligations. Whatever had started between the two of them had come to an untimely end.

He rubbed at the tension that had taken up residence at the back of his neck since the state police call had wakened him with the news of Davis and Becca's accident. He and Davis smiled from the silver-framed photo atop the bookcase, taken the day they'd won the tennis doubles cup. He'd never hear Davis laugh again, never enjoy the interplay of ideas as they planned a new project, never see Davis's joy in his baby daughter.

Something steeled inside him. All he could do now for his friend was to ensure Marcy's inheritance. All he could do to protect the life he'd built in Lakeview was to save the company. Everyone in town knew how quickly Frank had run through his inheritance from his father. He wouldn't let that happen to the company, for Marcy's sake and his own. If the only way to those aims was marrying Annie, so be it.

An image of Annie's stubborn face formed in his mind. Now he had to convince the bride.

Once, he'd been intrigued by that cool exterior of hers, wanting to know what lay behind it. He'd thought he was breaking through to her until everything blew up in the face of Davis's sudden decision to elope.

He might be able to reach Annie again, but that armor of hers was probably stronger than it had been before.

The phone rang, and he reached for it. He'd given Vera Rowland, their secretary-receptionist, the day off, assuming he'd get nothing accomplished so soon after the funeral.

"Link?"

Annie's voice sent him bolt upright in his chair. She sounded panic-stricken, and it took a lot to panic Annie Gideon.

"What is it? What's wrong?"

"Frank and Julia are here—" She choked on the words. "You'd better come."

"I'll be right there." He was on his feet as he said the words. "Hang on."

He covered the small outer office in a few strides and slammed out the door. Crossing the street, he jogged diagonally across the pocket-size park that formed Lakeview's town square. At this hour on a September afternoon the only occupants were a couple of mothers with strollers and two elderly men feeding the squirrels. The park, like the Conrad house, exuded stability, roots, belonging. All the things he hadn't had before he'd come to Lakeview. All the things he wouldn't give up.

The door was unlocked, and he didn't bother to knock. Apprehension carried him into the living room.

Annie clutched Marcy, with Frank and Julia pressing in on her. Embattled, she sent him a look of appeal mingled with relief. That must be some kind of first—for Annie to feel relief at the sight of him.

He moved toward them, feeling the balance of power shifting at his presence. Frank had obviously planned some sort of preemptive strike. Well, it wasn't going to work.

"Frank, Julia." He'd keep a polite demeanor if it killed him. Losing his temper with Frank would only play into the man's hands. "What are you doing here?"

Frank's smile didn't falter. "I told Annie there was no need to call you. This is family business."

"And I'm an outsider, I suppose. Annie did call me, so that means she wants me here."

Annie was putting up a good front, but fear filled her brown eyes. "They wanted Marcy."

He moved closer, putting his arm around her and the baby. She stiffened, then relaxed as if accepting that he was on her side.

He focused on her face, intent on erasing the fear. Frank shouldn't know she was afraid. "No one is taking Marcy. We won't let that happen."

"This is family business," Frank repeated. "As Davis's closest living relatives, my wife and I are the logical people to take care of little Marcy."

"And take care of little Marcy's inheritance, too, I suppose." His anger sparked.

Frank didn't seem affected by the accusation. "We're family," he repeated. "As you said, you're the outsider."

He tensed, but before he could say something he'd regret, Annie straightened.

"I'm Becca's sister. I'm the one she wanted to take

care of her child." The fire was back in Annie's eyes. "I won't let her down."

That fire seemed to bank Link's fury. Frank's attempt to take the child had wakened Annie to the danger they faced. That would work to his advantage in convincing her.

"I think a sister trumps a cousin, Frank. Maybe you and Julia better leave. You're not going to get what you want here."

"Choosing sides, are you? Maybe you should reconsider, Annie. We can give Marcy a real family. You want what's best for her, don't you?"

"I'm what's best for her." Her mouth set with a stubbornness he could have told Frank wouldn't be moved.

Maybe Frank recognized that fact. He shrugged, then gestured Julia toward the door. "Fine. We'll see you in court, then. I think you'll find Judge Carstairs will recognize the value of what we have to offer that little girl."

They swept out. He felt Annie sag with relief when the door closed. Then, as if she realized she was leaning against him, she took a step away.

"Down," Marcy said loudly, and Annie gave a weak laugh as she set the toddler on her feet.

"She was so still the whole time they were here. She must have sensed how scared I was." She met his eyes gravely. "Thank you, Link."

"I hate to say I told you so, but I did. Now do you understand?"

Annie's brown eyes clouded, and she crossed her arms protectively over her chest. "You were right about the Lesters."

"And I was right about what we have to do." Didn't she realize that? "If you want to keep that child, this is the only solution, and the sooner we do it the better. The Lesters are probably consulting their attorney as we speak. There'll be a hearing, and we'd better go into it married if we're going to have a chance."

"We have to see an attorney."

"Annie—"

Anger flared in her eyes, but behind it he saw vulnerability. "I'm not going off half-cocked, so you might as well get used to the idea. We see a lawyer first. Then—" She seemed to take a breath. "Well, then we'll see what's best."

He could say he already knew what was best, but he suspected that wasn't going to sway her. "I'll call Chet Longly. He's the lawyer the firm uses. Will he do, or do you want to find someone yourself?"

"He'll do." She shivered.

He nodded, picking up the phone. At least she seemed to accept that he was irrevocably involved in this. For once, she couldn't avoid him.

And that was just as well, because one way or another, he intended to marry her.

Chapter Two

Annie held the baby on her lap as she sat next to Link in the attorney's office the next morning, watching as every avenue of escape was blocked to her. Each word Chet Longly spoke seemed to make marriage to Link loom more inexorably.

She gazed past the attorney, trying to ease the sense of things closing in on her. His office, like every other important thing in the small town, faced the town square. Two days ago the flag at its center had hung at half-staff, in mourning for the funerals of two prominent citizens. Today the banner snapped in a brisk September breeze, colors bright in the sunshine.

Marcy wiggled, restless after a half hour's worth of adult conversation. Holding one arm around the baby's rounded middle, Annie reached into the diaper bag and pulled out one of the soft toys she'd tossed in before leaving the house. Maybe that would occupy Marcy for a moment at least.

Becca's next-door neighbor had offered to watch Marcy during the appointment, and she'd turned her down so quickly that it was a wonder the grandmotherly woman hadn't taken offense. After that episode with the Lesters, she was afraid to leave Marcy with anyone. Maybe there wasn't anyone in this town she could trust.

Well, probably the man who had been Davis's attorney was trustworthy. He'd been openly apologetic that he'd never succeeded in getting Davis to make a will. Davis, like so many people, hadn't thought there was any hurry.

Who would have expected the unthinkable?

Lord, why did this happen? Why Davis and Becca?

There wasn't any answer to that, just as there hadn't been any answer during the long night when she'd asked God whether this marriage was the right thing to do.

She shot a sideways glance at Link while the attorney patiently explained the ramifications of a custody hearing. Link's grave, composed face gave no hint to his feelings. He thought he already knew the only answer.

"So, as I say, there's no cut-and-dried solution." Chet Longly spread his hands, his open, friendly face troubled. "The judge has a great deal of discretion in a custody case. Even if you had written proof that Davis and Becca wanted you to take Marcy, the judge could decide against that. It's not likely, but it could happen."

Link stirred. "You agree that our case would be stronger if we were married."

"I can't advise you to marry in an effort to deceive the court." Chet said the words as if he walked on eggshells. "On the other hand, if you marry because you're fond of each other and because you want to provide security for a child you both love, I think that could tip the scales in your favor."

Link glanced at her, his dark eyes seeming to say he'd told her so.

Well, he couldn't blame her for exploring every possibility, could he? Knowing Link, he probably could. He'd never had much patience with her passion for details.

"Also, there's the fact that Ms. Gideon is living in the Conrad house, already taking care of the child," the attorney went on. "I hate to bring up the old saw about possession, but it does make the judge less likely to order a change that could be upsetting to the baby."

Link's jaw tightened. "I suspect that was what Frank had in mind yesterday. If he'd gotten his hands on Marcy—"

Annie suppressed the shudder that moved through her. In those frightening moments, when she'd actually feared the Lesters would snatch Marcy from her arms, she'd turned to Link.

She needed help. Hard though it was to accept, she couldn't do this alone.

"Either way, the best thing is to set up a hearing before the judge as quickly as possible, before the Lesters take any other action." The attorney stood, looking at them with concern in his face. "I'll leave you alone to discuss it for a few minutes."

He crossed the room, his footsteps making little sound on the plush carpet. The door closed softly behind him.

She had to stop collecting options and make a decision. However much she might have resented it in the past, she knew that Link's loyalty had always been to Davis. If that loyalty extended to his daughter, maybe that was all she could ask.

"It's not easy, is it."

She met Link's gaze, startled, to find that he was looking at her with sympathy.

"No." She tried to swallow the lump that refused to leave her throat in spite of the fact that she'd cried every tear she had to shed in the past few days. "I spent most of the night praying about it. Maybe this is the only answer, but how can I take vows I don't mean?"

Link's hand tightened to a fist on the polished mahogany arm of the chair. "Don't you think I have qualms about that?"

"I didn't know it mattered to you." She had assumed, when he'd stood next to her as godparents to the baby, that he believed, but she hadn't probed deeper than that.

"It does." He clipped the words off, his face grim. "You're not the only person to struggle with this, Annie."

She tried to smile. "Are you getting any answers?"

"I don't pretend to be a great theologian—"

He leaned toward her, and she felt the intensity of his belief reaching out to her.

"—but I *am* sure it would be a greater wrong to let that baby go to people who don't care about her than to marry for reasons other than love."

His words shot straight to her heart. She'd never expected to find the kind of all-consuming love Becca and Davis had. If marrying Link saved their baby, perhaps that was reason enough.

"If...if we do this, how long would our marriage have to last?"

Link frowned. "I don't know. But I'm not involved with anyone else, so I'm in no hurry. And from what Becca has said about you, I'm assuming you're not in a relationship right now, either."

The thought of Becca discussing her love life with Link left a bad taste in her mouth. Had her sister thought her an object of pity because she didn't have a husband and child?

"That's not really the point." She kept her voice cool. "I do have a life elsewhere."

"Once the judge grants custody to us, I don't see any reason why you couldn't go ahead with your plans to take Marcy back to Boston. After all, your parents are there and it would be logical for you to want to be near them. I'll stay here to manage the company. After a reasonable period of time, one of us can file for divorce.''

The image of her cozy apartment in Boston floated in front of Annie's eyes, a haven from the uncertainty and grief of the past days. She could take care of Marcy there without the constant reminders of her loss.

Marcy threw her black-and-white block, and it bounced harmlessly against the side of the desk. ''Down,'' she announced, wiggling her way off Annie's lap.

''Where are you going, little girl?'' Link caught her before she could grab the cord and pull the telephone to the floor. ''Here, have a look at this.'' He handed her his key ring, and Marcy gave him an enchanting smile.

''She has Davis's smile, you know that?'' He touched the baby's cheek lightly.

Annie glimpsed a sheen of tears in his dark eyes, and the sight disarmed her. It seemed to tear down some of the barricades she held against him.

''Yes, she does,'' she said softly.

Link cleared his throat, as if he felt the same tightness she did. ''Davis was my best friend. I owe it to him to take care of his child. I don't know anything about changing diapers, but I'll do my best to run the company properly and preserve her inheritance. I can't offer more than that.''

Oddly enough, that glimpse of his grief was reassuring. His concern might be primarily for the company, but it was for the baby's sake as well as his own.

Link looked at her, his eyebrows lifting in the question he'd been asking all along. ''Well, Annie?''

For Marcy, she told herself. *For Marcy.*

''All right.'' She had to force the words out. ''I'll marry you.''

It was his wedding day, and he was on his way to meet his bride. Link grimaced at his reflection in the rearview mirror. The three days they'd had to wait once they applied for the license had been an eternity. He'd been constantly on edge, sure something would go wrong—that Annie would back out, that Frank would launch some unexpected offense, anything.

So far, so good. The wedding was today, and the hearing before Judge Carstairs set for tomorrow. Chet seemed as optimistic as an attorney could be. With any luck, this time the next day they'd be safe.

And then? For a moment he couldn't see beyond the immediate goal. He shook his head. It was very simple. Annie would return to Boston with the baby, and he'd go back to running the company.

He drew up in front of the church and sat for a moment, staring out at the square. The gazebo glinted white through the surrounding trees. The maples, just beginning to change color, advertised the turning of the season. Tragedy happened, but life moved on.

Right now, moving on meant going through with this wedding. He and Annie had an agreement, just like any other business contract. As long as they kept the situation strictly business, no one would get hurt.

He glanced at the florist's box lying on the passenger seat and jeered at himself. He was breaking his own rules. He hadn't intended to do that but he'd found himself walking into the florist's. No matter what had prompted their wedding, a bride should have flowers.

An orchid hadn't seemed quite right for Annie, and the chrysanthemums the shop had in stock for the high school homecoming were out of the question. He'd settled for a small arrangement of yellow rosebuds, and their delicate aroma filtered through the white cardboard box. Hopefully the very idea of flowers wouldn't remind her of the funeral.

He caught sight of Chet, hovering outside the church, ready to be their witness. Now or never. He picked up the box, got out of the car and walked across to meet his best man.

"Still sure about this?" Chet raised his eyebrows. He was dressed, like Link, in a dark suit that seemed appropriate for an informal wedding.

"I'm sure." He pulled open the door to the church offices. "We made arrangements to have the ceremony in Pastor Laing's study instead of the sanctuary."

"Too many memories in there, I guess."

Link nodded, throat tightening again. Too many, and too recent.

The door to the pastor's study stood open. He stepped inside. Nora Evers, Davis and Becca's next-door neighbor, held Marcy. An improbable hat perched on Nora's white hair, and the baby was trying hard to pull off a purple flower.

"Nora, glad you could be here." They'd needed witnesses, and he'd felt the grandmotherly woman would add a touch of permanence to the proceedings.

Pastor Laing said something welcoming, but Link's attention was caught by Annie, standing unsmiling in front of the window. She wore a navy business suit with a white blouse, and her shiny brown hair curved in toward her rounded chin. Unlike Nora, she'd apparently seen no reason to wear a hat. She looked cool, severe and businesslike.

Once he'd been challenged by that cool exterior, but in the current circumstances he found it somehow reassuring. Annie looked as if nothing could touch her.

"I guess we should get started." Pastor Laing picked up a worn black worship book and came around the desk to stand in front of them, his face austere. "If you're both sure you're ready."

"We are," Link said. He handed Annie the florist's box.

She looked startled, then opened the box and took

out the roses. He couldn't see her expression, but she clutched the flowers tightly.

They'd talked with Garth Laing at length about this wedding, being carefully honest with him. Link certainly had no intention of lying to a man he respected as much as he did Garth. Maybe they'd left a few things out when they'd discussed their reasons for being married immediately, but if they had, he suspected someone as intuitive as the pastor could read between the lines.

Garth had agreed to marry them, that was the important thing. If they'd gone to a justice of the peace, he wasn't sure Annie's resolve would have held up.

Garth glanced from Link's face to Annie's. He nodded, as if satisfied with whatever he saw there. Then he began to read the age-old words of the wedding service.

Breathe, Link told himself. *All you have to do is remember your responses. That, and hope Annie doesn't say "I don't" instead of "I do."*

The preliminaries over, Garth smiled at them. "Please join hands."

For an instant he thought Annie wouldn't move. Then she extended her hand.

Her fingers were so cold it was like taking a handful of ice. He clasped her hand in his, trying to warm it, and Annie looked up at him.

Shock ran through him. All that cool composure of hers was a facade. For a moment, he saw the grief and vulnerability in her golden-brown eyes, and the sight shook him to the heart.

Beneath her controlled exterior, Annie was fragile, so fragile. She'd just undergone the most devastating experience of her life, and now she was plunged into something she wouldn't have dreamed possible a week earlier.

Dealing with Annie right now was like handling high explosives. One false move, and everything he'd naively thought was settled could blow sky high, leaving nothing but pieces.

Garth's voice paused, and Link realized he had to say his vows. Holding her hands in his, he began.

The ring felt odd on her finger. Annie stood at the dresser in the guest room at Becca's house, staring down at it. Her hand looked strange—the hand of a married woman.

She took a shaky breath. Hard as it was to believe, they'd actually done this thing. She and Link were husband and wife, legally and in God's sight.

Did we do the right thing, Father? We honestly tried to determine Your will. Surely it was worth any sacrifice to keep Marcy safe.

Annie knew she'd better finish changing her clothes and get back downstairs. She'd left Marcy with Link, and she wasn't sure how comfortable he was watching a lively toddler. Marcy's little hands could move at the speed of light when she wanted something, and Annie was already discovering that she needed faster reflexes to keep up with her.

She pulled on khakis and a camel sweater, ran a brush through her hair and decided that would have to do. On to the next thing.

She and Link had already decided they'd both stay in the house tonight, since they didn't want to raise any awkward questions with the hearing tomorrow. Link could sleep on the couch in Davis's office. Being here together was difficult, but it was only for a night.

Once the custody case was settled, the need to look like a married couple would be finished. She'd take Marcy home, and that would be that.

In the meantime, she could certainly cope with the situation for a day or two. This was business, and she knew how to handle business.

The thought comforted her. She went quickly out of the room and down the stairs.

She found Link and Marcy in the family room, where he was trying to dissuade the baby from pulling all the videos out of the cabinet.

"How about playing with the nice blocks, instead?" He sounded harassed.

"She likes just about anything better than her toys, according to Becca."

Link looked up at her from his prone position on the rug next to Marcy. A smile tilted his lips. "What do you suggest I do about it?"

She had to remind herself not to react to that smile. *Business.* She walked into the adjoining kitchen and pulled out the drawer her sister had filled with plastic containers and utensils.

"Look, Marcy. Look what Nan has." She tapped a wooden spoon invitingly on a plastic container.

Marcy dropped a video on Link's arm and trotted over to grab the spoon away from Annie. She plopped down in front of the drawer.

"Whatever anyone else has, that's what she wants. Becca called it the toddler's creed." Her smile faltered when she seemed to hear her sister's voice.

Link closed the video cabinet quickly, snapping the safety lock. "Nan? How did you get to be Nan?"

"Aunt Annie is a mouthful. She hasn't managed it yet."

He unfolded himself from the floor and walked toward her. Her mouth went suddenly dry. They were alone together. They were married.

He stopped, looking down at the baby. "Speaking of cooking utensils, have you given any thought to supper?"

She stared at him blankly. So much for the efficient, businesslike way she was going to handle things. "No, I guess I haven't." She hated admitting to any error. "It never entered my mind."

"Well, we have to eat. Why don't you grab a jacket, and I'll take the two of you out."

That just seemed to multiply her inefficiency. "Marcy's going to be tired out soon. I doubt she'd last through a restaurant dinner without a meltdown."

He looked at the baby with caution, as if anticipating an explosion. "I could pick up some take-out."

"The freezer's still full of the food people brought over for the funeral. I'll microwave something for tonight."

By tomorrow, she wouldn't need to feel responsible for Link's dinner.

"Okay." He sat down on the floor next to Marcy. "I'll keep an eye on her while you're doing that."

Having Link, in jeans and a dark blue sweater, taking up half the kitchen floor didn't seem conducive to getting a meal together quickly. Still, it would be worse if she were trying to do it with Marcy underfoot.

She pulled foil-covered dishes from the freezer, setting things onto the pale birch table. For an instant her vision blurred.

Everyone in town must have loved Becca and Davis. Their grief had found expression in their bringing more food than she and Link could possibly eat. It was just as well that she hadn't thought of cooking anything else.

When the table was set with the floral pottery dishes and blue-and-white napkins, she scooped Marcy up. "Supper time, sweetpea. Let's see what you like."

Marcy liked just about everything until halfway through the meal, when she suddenly decided she didn't like anything. She wailed, then began rubbing her eyes, depositing a generous helping of macaroni and cheese in her hair in the process.

Annie glanced at Link, placidly eating a second helping of ham and scalloped potato casserole. "I'd better get her ready for bed."

He nodded, then came around the table to plant a kiss on Marcy's cheek, adroitly avoiding the waving, sticky hands. "Do you want me to carry her upstairs?"

"I can handle her." She mopped the baby's face and hands quickly. She'd better be able to handle Marcy. From now on, that would be her primary responsibility. For just an instant the thought frightened her, but she shook it off. She could do this. She had to. Nobody loved Marcy more than she did.

A wet half hour later she held a rosy-cheeked cherub, dressed for bed in pajamas dotted with yellow giraffes that matched the wallpaper. The elephant lamp cast a soft glow over the nursery.

Marcy looked adorable. She suspected that she hadn't fared so well. Her hair fell damply in her face and her sweater sported several wet patches. She looked up at a sound to find Link standing in the doorway, watching them.

"Come to help?"

He ambled toward them, looking entirely too dry and perfect. "Came to say good-night."

He held out his hands to Marcy. She leaned coyly against Annie's shoulder for an instant, then lunged into his arms, chortling.

Link lifted her over his head, laughing up at her. The laughter transformed his face from its earlier bleakness. Annie's heart lurched.

"Let's see if we can get her into bed without a struggle," she said.

This was the moment that had been difficult each night. Marcy, who normally went to bed without a peep, had been clingy and reluctant.

Link hugged the child, then swung her into the white crib, snuggling her down next to the soft, white, stuffed dog. Marcy lay still for an instant, then popped up again. She looked from one to the other of them, her blue eyes very round.

"Mama?" she asked tentatively. "Mama?"

Annie blinked back tears. "It's all right, sweetheart. Nan is here."

Link leaned over the crib railing, patting her. "You go to sleep now, darling. Link and Nan are here. We're not going to leave."

Marcy's eyes clouded up, as if tears weren't far off. He patted her again, humming in a soft bass. While Annie held her breath, Marcy lay down, pulling the dog close and slipping her thumb into her mouth. In a moment her eyes had closed.

Link straightened slowly. The movement brought him brushing against her as they stood side by side, looking down at the baby. The room was so silent she could hear Link's slow, steady breathing. She could almost imagine she heard the beating of his heart. Her own seemed to be fluttering erratically.

She took a breath, trying to steady herself. It was certainly a good thing this marriage was going to be a long-distance one. Because she didn't think she could cope with too much time spent in close quarters with her new husband.

Chapter Three

Gratitude mingled with her apprehension as Annie walked toward the courthouse the next day. She'd expected to be accompanied by only Link and the attorney. She'd thought she'd feel very much the outsider in the redbrick courthouse that was one of a row of similar buildings—town hall, public library, courthouse—that lined one side of the square.

Instead, Pastor Laing had turned up at the house early, saying he thought they might need moral support at such a difficult time. And Nora Evers, hat firmly in place on her white hair, had marched out of her house to join them.

The support helped, especially after the mostly sleepless night she'd endured. She'd been so aware of her responsibility for Marcy that even putting the baby monitor next to her pillow wouldn't relieve her concerns.

She shouldn't try to fool herself. Some of her sleeplessness had to be chalked up to Link's presence in the house as her husband. *Husband.* The word reverberated in her thoughts. That had to have been one of the strangest wedding nights in history.

She hadn't expected anything else. Of course not, she assured herself quickly. This was a business arrangement, not a marriage. That fact hadn't lessened her awareness of Link's presence. Even after his bedroom door had closed, her awareness had remained. Maybe soon, she'd get used to it. Maybe.

"Are you okay?" Link, carrying the baby, glanced at her as their little procession crossed the street.

Was she? "My stomach feels like I'm walking into an IRS audit without my notes."

His smile flickered. "As bad as that?"

She nodded. "What if…"

Link took her hand in a reassuring grip. "Let's not venture into what-ifs, not until we have to. That's what we have an attorney for."

"That's right." Chet mounted the three steps to the courthouse's double doors and held one side open for them. He smiled, but Annie thought she detected tension in him, as well. Maybe Chet wasn't as confident of the outcome as he'd like them to believe.

She entered the tiled, echoing hallway. Ahead of her a cluster of people stepped into the elevator— Frank, Julia and a woman who was probably their attorney. Her heart jolted.

Please, Lord, be with us this morning. We are do-

ing the right thing, aren't we? Don't let them take Marcy away.

Link's tension vibrated through the hand that clasped hers.

"Looks as if they're not giving up easily." His grip tightened.

"We didn't expect them to, did we." Now it was her turn to try and sound reassuring. She didn't feel assured. She felt panic-stricken.

"I guess not." Link waited until the door had closed and the elevator was carrying the Lesters upward before pushing the button.

"Do you think the judge knows the Lesters?" That was probable, given how small the town was. Maybe this would be over before it began, a victim of the Lakeview old boys' network.

"Judge Carstairs knows everyone in town," Chet said, answering the question before Link could say anything. "But that doesn't mean she won't be fair. After all, she's always dealing with people she knows."

Somehow she hadn't been thinking of the judge as a woman. She didn't know whether to be reassured by that or not. Would it make any difference in the way Judge Carstairs viewed a custody case?

She worried at it all the way up in the elevator, into the courtroom with its lofty ceiling and murals of Revolutionary War scenes, right into her seat behind a polished table. The judge's bench rose intimidatingly, towering above them.

She'd pictured someone elderly and severe, but Judge Carstairs couldn't have been more than fifty. Her glossy dark hair swung around a face that was discreetly made up, and the hand that wielded the gavel sported polished nails.

The judge looked down at the papers in front of her, then questioningly from one attorney to the other. "I thought this was a routine custody hearing for a minor child."

The Lesters' attorney stood. "Frank Lester and his wife contest awarding custody to the aunt, Your Honor. As you may be aware, Mr. Lester is the cousin of the child's father."

Judge Carstairs frowned. "What I may be aware of isn't pertinent, Counselor." She nodded toward the door at the side of the courtroom. "Let's move this into my chambers."

Annie sent a startled glance at Chet, who shrugged. "She does things her way," he murmured. "All we can do is go along."

They trooped out of the courtroom and into a book-lined room that looked like an elegant library in a private home. The judge took a seat behind the desk and waved them all to chairs. She glanced at Pastor Laing. "Garth, are you here to testify in this case?"

"I'm here as little Marcy's pastor," he said, sitting down next to Link. "I'm concerned that we do what's best for her, that's all."

The judge's dark gaze rested on him for a moment, then she nodded.

Annie tried to find something hopeful in that. The pastor's body language put him in their camp. She didn't know what they'd done to deserve that, but she was grateful.

"All of us want what's best for the child." Judge Carstairs's face softened in a smile as she glanced at Marcy, sitting contentedly on Link's lap.

Annie moved the diaper bag a little closer to her side. She'd come prepared with crackers, a pacifier, a cup of milk, a book, toys. The last thing they needed was for Marcy to have a cranky spell in the middle of this hearing.

"So," the judge continued, "we're going to have a nice, informal little conversation about the situation and try to figure out what that best is."

"Your Honor..." the Lesters' attorney began.

Judge Carstairs frowned. "You have some objection to that, Ms. Marshall?"

"No, Your Honor. But I'd like to point out that my clients haven't had an opportunity to prepare their case. This has come up very suddenly. Naturally, as the deceased's closest living relatives, they expected the child would come to them. They're a married couple, they're lifelong members of the community and Mr. Lester has an interest in the deceased's company."

Indignation flooded through Annie. The woman was talking as if only Davis's death had any significance.

Then she realized the judge was looking right at her.

"You have something to say, Ms.—" She glanced down at the file in front of her. "Ms. Gideon, is it?"

Annie felt the pressure of Link's hand clasping hers. "I'm Ann Gideon Morgan," she said firmly. "My sister, Becca Conrad, was the baby's mother. I've been taking care of Marcy since the accident, and I believe my husband and I are the logical people to continue to do so."

My husband and I. It was the first time she'd used the phrase, and it sounded odd to her ears. She could only hope that feeling wasn't obvious to the others in the room.

The judge's gaze moved from her face to Link's with what seemed to be a sharpening of interest. Annie's nerves clenched. What was the woman going to ask her? If she asked about the circumstances of their wedding, what could she say?

"Your Honor, this marriage—"

The judge cut Frank's words short with a sharp gesture. "This proceeding is informal, as I said. But I still ask the questions." She turned back to Annie. "Your marriage was rather sudden, wasn't it? Will you tell me how it came about?"

Please, let me say the right thing.

At some level she was ashamed to be clinging so tightly to Link's hand, but she couldn't seem to let go.

"I've known Link for over eight years." She could

only be surprised that she sounded so calm. "We were both very close to my sister and her husband. After the—" Her voice caught suddenly and she had to pause before she could continue. "After the accident, we felt the best thing for the baby we both love was to be married. Pastor Luing conducted the ceremony yesterday."

"I see." Her gaze rested thoughtfully on them. "Mr. Morgan, do you have anything to add?"

Link's hand twitched, but she was the only one to know that.

"Only that no one could be a better mother to this little girl than Annie, Your Honor."

He looked down at Marcy as he spoke, and she smiled up at him as if she understood. Then she turned to Annie, holding out her hands commandingly. "Nan," she said.

Annie lifted Marcy onto her lap, feeling a wave of love. Surely the judge would see how much she cared, wouldn't she?

Judge Carstairs folded her hands on the desk in front of her. "I think I've heard as much as I need to hear at this time."

At this time? The words sounded an alarm in Annie's mind.

"Your Honor, we haven't had an opportunity to present our case," Frank's attorney said.

"You've already pointed out that you haven't had time to prepare your case," Judge Carstairs said.

"I'm not inclined to take the child out of an established relationship."

A wave of relief swept Annie.

"However, I'm also not going to make a decision that affects the future of a child in a hurry."

Annie looked at Chet, but if he knew what the judge had in mind, his face didn't show it.

"Therefore, in the matter of the infant child Marcy Amanda Conrad, I'm ordering that she remain in the custody of her aunt and uncle, Ann and Lincoln Morgan, until such time as a full custody hearing can be held." She frowned at a calendar on her desk. "We'll set a hearing date in a month's time. That will allow both sides to prepare their arguments and also allow Children's Services to conduct an evaluation of the home Mr. and Mrs. Morgan are providing. The Lesters will have visitation, also observed by Children's Services. That's all."

Annie sank back in her chair. She could vaguely hear Frank protesting, being hushed by his attorney. Link seemed to be saying something to Chet. All she could do was try and take it in.

There was no decision, either for or against them. She forced herself to look at Link. His set face probably hid feelings as appalled and shocked as hers.

She wouldn't be going back to Boston with Marcy today. She'd spend the next four weeks living in Lakeview with Link, trying to pretend to the world that they were just like any other newly married couple. And knowing that at any moment a social worker could decide she wasn't doing a good enough job and take Marcy away from her.

Link stirred restlessly in the leather chair in the family room. It was a comfortable chair, but he couldn't seem to find comfort at the moment. What he wanted to do was throw on some shorts and go for a run, then go back to his quiet apartment.

He couldn't. Because of the judge's ruling, he was stuck here, trying to figure out how he and Annie were going to deal with this situation for the next month.

Chet had come over for a conference after they'd gotten Marcy to bed—a council of war was more like it. He'd been cautiously optimistic about the results of the hearing.

"...wouldn't have given you even temporary custody if she hadn't felt you were the right people to have Marcy," he was saying reassuringly.

Impossible to tell if Annie felt reassured. She sat very erect in the bentwood rocking chair, still and collected. The Annie who had gripped his hand so tightly during the hearing was submerged beneath that composed exterior she wore so well.

For an instant he felt annoyed with her for not showing more distress at the way things had blown up in their faces. Talk about irrational. Would he be happier if she were having hysterics? It was just as well that Annie kept her feelings to herself, given the situation they were in.

Chet glanced at him. "As far as I can see, the best thing the two of you—well, the three of you—can do is stay right here in Davis and Becca's house. It comes to Marcy anyway, and I'm sure it was the judge's intention that she not be moved."

Link gave a wistful thought to his small apartment, then dismissed it. He nodded toward the bright plastic slide and playhouse in the backyard, visible through the French doors of the family room. "We certainly couldn't fit that into my place. And I doubt Annie would like my decor."

A sudden smile broke through the somber expression on Annie's face. "Becca said it was decorated in early motel."

"Actually it's the furniture that was there when I moved in. I always thought someday I'd get around to having a house of my own."

But not Davis's house. It didn't feel right to be sitting in this warm family room without Davis opposite him.

"That's settled, then," Chet said. "You'll stay here, carry on like any normal family."

"We need to talk about the company." That probably sounded abrupt, but he had to know where they stood.

Chet glanced toward Annie, probably thinking he wouldn't want to discuss this in front of her. "I could meet you at the office tomorrow."

"No. Annie's just as involved as I am in this situation. It's Marcy's future we're talking about, after all." Again he pictured Davis sitting in the chair opposite him. Protecting Marcy's future meant protecting the company.

Annie stirred. "I know you said that Frank had bought a share in the company. But I don't understand why anything would change now that Davis is gone."

"Originally, Davis and I were equal partners." He clenched the chair arms. "Actually, he put up most of the start-up money, but he insisted on a partnership." Most of the Conrad fortune was gone by that time, but there was still enough for Davis to invest in their futures. "Then when we wanted to expand, we divided the pot. Davis and I each owned thirty percent of the company. The remaining forty percent was split among four investors—Frank, Delbert Conrad—Davis's great-uncle, and two friends of his father, Harvey Ward and old Doc Adams. Davis was company president, I was chairman."

"Davis's share goes to Marcy, but with the custody still not settled..." Annie let her voice trail off.

"Exactly. It leaves us in limbo. Davis and I would vote together on any decision, and together we had a majority." He didn't want to voice what he'd been thinking, but he forced himself to. "Even without Marcy's shares, Frank could outvote me if he got the rest of the board on his side. With Marcy's share, all he'd need is his great-uncle's vote for complete control."

She leaned forward in the rocker. "But why would

he want it? He doesn't know anything about building, does he?"

"No." Chet answered for him. "Frank manages the rental properties he inherited and sits on the boards of a few institutions. He likes running things. And there's that lakefront property. He's said more than once that it's a potential gold mine, and I've had the impression lately that his expensive tastes are out-running his income." He stood. "All I can say is that you should continue the way you are. The rest of the board won't rush into any changes. I certainly wouldn't advise it."

Link stood, too, holding out his hand. "Thanks, Chet. For everything."

Annie joined him as Chet moved to the door. "Yes, thank you." She managed a smile. "I don't know how we'd have gotten through today without you."

"Just doing my job."

They stood together like any married couple saying good-night to a visitor. Was that what Annie was thinking, too? How were they going to do this, especially with a social worker looking over their shoulders, taking note of every mistake?

He closed the door, realizing that thought had been lurking at the back of his mind ever since the judge's ruling. Annie, with her nice, stable, middle-class up-bringing, couldn't possibly guess what terrors the threat of a social worker raised in his mind.

They'll take you away and put you in a home. His mother's voice, slurred with alcohol, sounded in his memory. Those were the words she'd always used when he got too much for her to handle.

At five or six, he hadn't understood what she meant, but it had terrified him enough to keep him in line through yet another move to yet another rented room in another town that didn't welcome them....

"Do you want anything to eat?" Annie gestured toward the kitchen.

"No." He didn't realize how sharply that had come out until he saw anger flare in her eyes.

"If you think I should have produced a six-course dinner after a day like this—"

"No, of course not. I'm sorry. I wasn't even thinking about food."

She looked a bit mollified. "What were you thinking about? The company?"

"Not exactly." She didn't need to know he was remembering a childhood she couldn't begin to imagine. "Just all we have to do to make this work."

Annie rubbed her forehead, as if the very idea gave her a headache. "Home visits, social workers. How do you prepare for something like that?"

That was certainly the last thing he wanted to discuss. "We'd better start with telling your parents what's going on. I know your father's worried. And then there's your job. You'd better apply for a leave of absence."

He stopped, realizing that Annie no longer looked tired. She just looked mad.

"We?" she said pointedly. "It sounds to me as if all those things concern me, not you."

He picked up her hand, touching the plain gold band on her finger. "Married, remember? We have to start acting that way."

"That doesn't mean you need to tell me what to do." She yanked her hand away. "But then, you're really good at telling people what to do, aren't you."

Something seemed to snap inside him. "Are you still talking about the past? Get over it, Annie. We've got more important things to handle now."

"Definitely more important. And that reminds me that I couldn't trust you once before."

He put his fists on his hips, glaring at her. All the things he'd wanted to say for years bubbled up inside him. Only now, he didn't have any reason to keep them back. Everyone involved in his original promise was gone.

"It wasn't a matter of trust," he said evenly. "I made a promise."

"A promise to do what? Keep Davis safe from unworthy females like Becca?"

He could only stare at her. Of course that was what she thought. He hadn't given her any other possibilities.

"It wasn't that. Don't ever think that. Becca was probably the best thing that ever happened to Davis." *As you were to me.* His first love had come back to haunt him. "It was Davis, not Becca. His parents made me promise to look out for him that summer."

Her chin set firmly. "Did they expect you to keep him from falling in love?"

"No." He took a breath, knowing it was time to speak. "They expected me to keep him from acting irrationally. Davis had bipolar disorder. They didn't want him doing anything rash while he was in a manic phase. I was supposed to prevent that."

"Bipolar disorder?" She looked up at him, and he could see the wheels turning in her mind, trying to make sense of the term. "Well, for goodness' sake, why make such a big secret out of it? It's nothing to be ashamed of."

"You know that. I know that. But Davis's parents never coped with it very well, and at the time, there was more of a stigma attached to it. And the least change in Davis's routine could trigger a problem."

"And Becca was a trigger?" She flared up again, anger making her eyes bright. "You should have told me. You should have told Becca! She certainly had a right to know."

"I couldn't. Will you get that through your head? I knew it was dumb, but I'd promised to keep it a secret, and I keep my promises."

Quite suddenly the anger in her eyes was drowned by tears. "Becca never told me. She did mention stress a few times, when Davis didn't come with her on a visit, but she never explained. All these years I thought we shared everything, and she never told me about it."

He felt helpless in the face of her tears. "She probably never thought it was necessary."

"Necessary? I was her sister!"

He certainly had a gift for making a bad situation worse. "I mean, she probably didn't even think about it as a problem. His medication was so much better in recent years that it rarely became an issue. I worked with him every day, and I'd nearly forgotten about it."

Annie brushed tears from her cheeks. "I thought—" She stopped, shook her head. "I'm sorry. It's ridiculous to be falling apart over that now."

Sympathy welled up in him. No, not sympathy. Empathy. He knew exactly what she was feeling, because he felt it, too. They were both being blindsided by grief.

He touched her cheek gently, wiping away a tear. "I don't think that's why, is it? But if it helps, go ahead and be mad at me."

Her sudden smile knocked him off balance. "Can I really?"

He was being drawn into that smile. He couldn't help himself. All the warmth Annie hid behind her cool exterior blazed in it, drawing him closer and closer.

His wife. The words seemed to twitch a chord inside him. Annie was his wife. He'd thought he was immune to what that phrase represented. He wasn't.

That sham wedding night had been bad enough. He'd seen the wariness in Annie's face as she'd said good-night and scurried up the stairs. He'd deliberately stayed downstairs, giving her time to settle, aware of every footstep overhead, every creak of the bed.

Then she'd been at a safe distance. Now she was inches away, her warmth drawing him closer and closer.

Oh, no. He drew back, his hand dropping away from her face. No, indeed. This business of marriage was going to be difficult enough as it was. If he let himself give in to that surge of attraction for Annie, it would be impossible.

Chapter Four

Oh, Becca, why didn't you tell me about Davis's problem? I thought we told each other everything, Annie thought as she looked at the photograph on the bookshelf. Becca, Davis and Marcy smiled at each other in the pewter frame. Their love fairly radiated into the room, catching at her heart.

Well, if she were being honest, she hadn't actually thought that—not since Becca married Davis. Certainly a married couple would have secrets they shared only with each other.

A chill seemed to touch her spine, like the frost that would soon claim the flowers Becca had planted alongside the house. She and Link were a married couple now, but the only secret they shared was the reason for that marriage.

She straightened the picture gently, then dropped the paper she was carrying on the end table next to the leather couch. She crossed to the French doors and looked out at the enclosed play yard.

Rain pelted down, as it had all day. It glistened on the red plastic slide and soaked into Marcy's sandbox, turning the sand from beige to brown. She traced a droplet that shivered down the pane as she thought about that wave of feeling that had swept over her when Link touched her cheek the night before, wiping her tears away.

Forget it, she told herself fiercely. It had been a temporary aberration, a moment of empathy in their shared grief—it had meant nothing. It wouldn't come again, because she wouldn't let it. This whole situation was difficult enough without letting emotion get out of control.

She didn't do that, ever. She was run by her head, not her heart. *Except perhaps that once…*

The *click* of the side door cut off a line of thought she'd rather not pursue.

Link paused, peeling off his windbreaker and shaking it outside before coming in. He eyed her with what she suspected was caution, probably no more eager than she was to venture into the emotional territory they'd found themselves in the previous night.

She pinned a smile to her face. ''You're home earlier than I expected. Marcy's still napping.''

He nodded, hanging his jacket on the closet hook. ''Too wet for most of what we planned to do at the site today. I sent the men home early.'' Something that might have been worry darkened his eyes for an instant. "Hope we don't have to do that too often. We need to get those houses under roof before the weather turns."

Of course he was worried about the job. She'd learned enough in the past few days to guess that the company was overextended where this new project was concerned.

"Accountants don't have to worry about the weather. Just tax season."

He nodded, then turned a questioning look on her. "Speaking of that, have you talked to your boss about taking a leave?"

"Not yet." The words came out more sharply than she had intended, and Link couldn't know she was annoyed at herself, not him. The step was necessary, but she'd put it off all day, as if to hold back the moment at which her life in Boston would come to a halt.

Link's square jaw seemed to get a bit squarer. "You know that has to be done. If Frank's attorney looks into your situation, she can't find that you're holding on to a job in Boston."

It didn't help her disposition in the least to know he was absolutely right. "I said I'd take care of it." She put her hand on the phone. "I'll do it right now."

"Fine," he said brusquely. "I'm going up to shower."

He stalked out of the room before she could say anything else. Not that she'd intended to apologize, had she? After all, this was her concern, not his.

Her mind replayed that moment when he'd lifted her hand, touching the gold band on her finger. *We're married, remember? We'd better start acting that way.*

Before she could think too much about that, she picked up the phone and punched in the number of the Boston firm that was about to lose her services. As the phone rang, a flicker of doubt assailed her. If she'd just had a baby, they'd have given her maternity leave without question. But in this case…

Fifteen minutes later she hung up, feelings divided between relief and regret.

"What's wrong?" Link's voice startled her. "Did they give you a hard time about the leave?"

She turned, shaking her head, and her breath caught. He stood in the doorway, clearly fresh from the shower. His dark hair lay damp against his head, curling slightly at his neck. His white polo shirt clung to his broad shoulders, as if he hadn't bothered to dry himself completely before pulling it on.

She had to turn away so he wouldn't notice her staring. She wasn't going to let herself be affected by him, remember?

"Actually, they couldn't have been nicer. My boss insisted on paying me through the end of the month, and my job will be waiting for me, no matter how long it takes."

"Sounds as if they consider you a valuable employee."

She heard him cross the room as he spoke, sensed

him stop behind her. She kept her gaze glued to the white phone on the bar between the kitchen and family room, as if it were about to ring.

"They do. I am."

"Then, why were you staring at the phone as if you were going to cry?"

"I wasn't." She glanced up at him in surprise, then regretted it. He stood very close, his dark eyes intent.

"Yes, you were." He frowned. "Look, I know it's going to be hard just to stay home with Marcy when you're used to a challenge every day, but we agreed this was the only option until the custody hearing."

"Trust me, being home with Marcy will be a challenge." She smiled, but felt the expression fade almost at once. "It's not that. It's just—"

"What?" His voice lowered to a rumble, soft as the patter of rain against the window. The room was so still she could hear the steady sound of his breath.

She rubbed her arms with her hands, suddenly chilled. "I've been in that job for seven years. That's who I am. Just as Becca was the wife and mother. Now everything's turned upside down."

He put his hand on her shoulder as if to reassure her, and she felt his warmth through the soft knit of her turtleneck.

"You'll do a good job. Marcy loves you, that's the important thing."

He didn't understand, and she didn't think she could make him.

"I love Marcy. That doesn't mean I shouldn't

worry about giving up something I do very well for something I probably won't do well at all."

His hand fell away from her shoulder, as if he'd expended all the sympathy he had to spare at the moment. "I think you're worrying unnecessarily."

Her skin was cold where his palm had been, and a tiny spark of anger flared. "How would you feel if it were your job that had to be sacrificed?"

All in an instant the atmosphere in the room changed. She felt his tension as if they touched—felt it pounding through his muscles and along his nerve endings. His eyes darkened.

"It's not." The flat words admitted no argument. "I run the company. It's not a job. It's my life."

The crevice between them widened into a chasm. *It's my life.*

She'd known the company was important to him. She hadn't known how important.

The chill she'd felt seemed to spread to her heart. She'd told herself it was good, for Marcy's sake, that he cared so much about the company.

But she was in a situation where she had to trust him, and she couldn't forget that he'd been willing to put aside her feelings once before when it came between him and something he valued.

What might Link do now if he thought he had to in order to save the company?

Link pulled his pickup into the driveway a few hours later, the flat white box on the seat next to him filling the cab with the aroma of cheese, pepperoni and tomato sauce. The pizza wasn't exactly a peace offering, but Annie *had* been upset. An unhappy Annie wasn't part of his plan to present a cheerful family face to anyone who was interested.

He shouldn't have snapped at her, but how could she possibly compare her job with what the company meant to him? Irritation sizzled along his nerves again. Her job, no matter how much her employer valued her, was just that—a job.

Annie had no way of knowing what his place in Lakeview meant to him, and she never would. The company was his life.

He looked back grimly at how far he'd come. The grubby kid who'd been an outsider in one town after another, living in one cheap dump after another, didn't exist any longer. Lakeview was home now, and no one in town knew about that kid who hadn't been welcomed anywhere.

People here respected him. They considered him one of them. Maybe part of that was thanks to Davis and his family, but most had resulted from his own hard work in building Conrad and Morgan into a company that brought good things to the town's economy. He wouldn't give up that respect and belonging, which meant he'd do what was necessary to save the company.

So the pizza probably was a peace offering. He and Annie had to get this marriage thing back to a safe, rational business footing, with no erratic flashes of emotion ruffling the surface.

He turned off the motor and grabbed the box. The past few days had been stressful for both of them. Starting now, he would set the standard for the calm, friendly relationship that would help them get what they wanted most.

It shouldn't be hard. Knowing Annie, she was as eager as he to keep things on an even keel between them. Balancing the pie—half pepperoni for him, half broccoli for her—he ducked quickly through the drizzle to the family room door.

The door opened on a scene considerably more chaotic than the one he'd left. Marcy happily pulled books from the bookshelves he and Davis had built, while Annie tried to restrain the baby with one hand and juggle a book she was reading with the other.

He slid the pizza box onto the counter and scooped Marcy up in his arms, earning a giggle as he swung her high. "Hey, little girl, you don't need all those books, do you?"

Annie gave him an absent glance and returned to her book. "I'll clean them up later. I wanted to check on something before you got back."

He tipped up the front of the volume she held. "*The Toddler Years.* What's so important you have to look it up right this minute?"

"I'm trying to find out if it's okay to give Marcy pizza." Her forehead wrinkled. "I'm sure the book covers that somewhere."

He snapped the book shut, trying to hide his amusement. "You should have been a librarian."

"There's nothing wrong with looking up the answers to questions." She led the way to the kitchen, her shoulders stiff.

"No, there's not," he said quickly. *Don't ruffle her feathers, remember?* "It's just that I've been here when Marcy ate pizza. She loves it."

"Oh." She looked as if she was struggling to be grateful. "Thanks."

She didn't like the fact that he knew something about Marcy that she didn't. Scary, that he knew so easily what she was thinking.

He slid Marcy into the high chair while Annie snapped a bib around her neck. She put the pizza carton in the center of the table, and they sat down opposite each other. While he was out, she'd set the table with bright blue place mats and flowered dishes, reminding him painfully of the times he'd eaten here with Davis and Becca.

Annie took Marcy's hand, then reached across to him tentatively with her other hand. "Davis and Becca always held hands when they asked the blessing," she said. "I thought we should keep that up."

"Good idea." He clasped the hand she offered, wrapping his fingers around hers. For some reason, it made him think of that moment in the pastor's study when they'd held hands and become husband and wife. "Will you, or shall I?"

"I will." Annie's fingers tightened on his as she

bowed her head. "Dear Lord, we thank You for the blessings of this day. Please bless this food, and make us fit stewards of this dear child. Amen."

"Amen," he echoed softly.

The moment of prayer seemed to restore Annie's good humor. She cut a small wedge of pizza for Marcy, then smiled when the baby shoved it eagerly in her mouth.

"Looks as if you were right."

"Thanks for admitting it." He helped himself to a wedge, relieved. She sounded normal, and that was what he wanted. No unexpected emotions on either side. They were just two people, partners in a difficult job, cooperating.

Her smile peeped through. "Okay, I guess I'm pretty obvious." She handed Marcy another small piece. "But becoming a parent is scary. I feel as if everyone knows more than I do about it."

"You're not having regrets about doing this, are you?"

"No!" The word leaped from her mouth. "Nobody could love Marcy more than I do. Nobody!" Love filled her expression.

He leaned back, a little shaken. Love that fierce was humbling. He hadn't expected that from Annie— hadn't realized the emotional strength that filled her where the child was concerned.

All right, this wasn't strictly a business deal. Still, his job was to run the company and keep Marcy's inheritance safe.

He'd leave the emotional end of things to Annie. She'd have to manage that on her own.

"I'm going to prove it to you." Link pulled a heavy photo album from the bookshelf and sat down next to her on the black leather couch, opening it. "You'll see that I'm right."

Annie leaned back, smiling a little. She was ready to forgive Link for knowing more than she had about Marcy's ability to eat pizza. And she was so relieved that the baby had gone peacefully to bed without tears or asking for Mama that she was willing to go along with Link's typical determination to prove he was right.

Their disagreement of the moment was over whether Marcy looked more like her mother or her father. Link, convinced she resembled Davis as a child, had pulled out the Conrad family photo albums to show her.

Well, given all the things they'd disagreed about, this was a fairly benign one. A good thing, too. They'd set off entirely too many explosions in each other over the past few days. She'd let Link past her emotional guard too often. She had to find a way of dealing with the situation without that.

Link looked down at the faded photos as he paged his way through the book that had belonged to Davis's parents. His dark hair, usually under such strict control, had become tousled, making him look younger. Absorbed in the album, he seemed relaxed, as if the strain of his grief and his worry over the building project had temporarily been dismissed.

"There. Look at that." Link, grinning, pointed to a photo of a diaper-clad baby proudly holding himself upright against a piano bench.

Annie recognized the bench—it still stood at the spinet in the living room. She bent to look closer and her hand brushed Link's, setting off a wave of warmth. She moved her fingers away carefully and tried to concentrate on the picture.

"Well, there's a little resemblance, I guess," she conceded.

"A little? She's the image of her daddy." Link leafed through the pages, apparently oblivious to that touch. "Let me find another one."

"No fair." She pulled the album toward her. "You're not letting me see all of them."

He smiled, letting half of the heavy pages rest on her lap. "Go ahead, look. You'll see the same resemblance in every picture."

"We'll see." She turned pages. Davis with his parents, who'd been gone for five years now. They'd died within a year of each other—his father from cancer, his mother from heart failure, as if she hadn't wanted to go on without her husband.

Davis in a Scouts uniform…a football uniform. The story of his life was played out in the series of photos.

She touched one of Davis in a graduation gown.

"It looks as if his illness didn't keep him from participating in plenty of activities."

"Pictures can be deceiving." Link flattened his hand against the page, and his voice had gone flat, too. "He spent several weeks in a hospital during his senior year."

She leaned back against the buttery-soft leather, watching his face. "You didn't know him then, did you?"

He shook his head. "We met in college, freshman year. Roommates by the luck of the draw. His mother told me about it later." He flipped another page or two. "There. That's Christmas break our freshman year."

Again, she recognized the setting—the living room of this house. Davis's mother, elegant and composed, stood in front of a Christmas tree, flanked by Davis and Link.

Link had been thinner then, as if he hadn't yet caught up with his height. He looked—she tried to find the right word. Happy, but somehow almost surprised at that happiness, as if thinking it didn't belong to him.

"You didn't go home to your family?" She ventured the question cautiously, remembering that he seldom spoke of his people.

"No." The curt monosyllable closed the door on that subject. "Davis's parents invited me to Lakeview with him." He touched the picture gently. "His parents made me so welcome. I'd never had a Christmas like that.''

She wanted to ask why he hadn't gone to his own home, what his other Christmases had been like, but his attitude had already warned her off the subject of his family.

''I never really got to know Davis's parents well. They seemed very nice.''

Nice. The truth was, she'd always felt uneasy around them, always mindful of the fact that they hadn't wanted their son to marry Becca.

''They treated me like one of their own. I don't think I could ever repay their kindness.''

''You tried.'' She regretted the words the instant they were out. Why did she want to spoil the momentary harmony between them by bringing up something on which they'd never agree?

Link's jaw tightened, a tiny muscle twitching. ''I made a promise. I told you that.''

''I know. I'm sorry.'' Instinctively, without thinking, she put her hand over his. ''Really. I shouldn't have said that. I realize you were doing what you thought you had to.''

And whatever had begun between us didn't measure in the balance with what you thought you owed them.

She couldn't say that, of course. But she couldn't help thinking that perhaps Davis's parents had used Link's sense of obligation to put a burden on him that wasn't rightfully his.

Link's fingers closed around hers. "They were kind to me, and Davis was my best friend. I'd have done anything for him then." His fingers tightened. "And I'd do anything now for that little girl, because she's Davis's child. You know you can trust me on that, don't you?"

Trust. He'd put his finger right on the root of her uncertainty.

"I know you'll do all you can for Marcy because of Davis," she said carefully. He'd let her down before, but this time they were on the same side, weren't they? "I'd like to think you can love her for herself, too."

He stared down at their clasped hands, and his shuttered face hid his thoughts. "I love her," he said. "The reason doesn't matter. I'll keep her inheritance safe, no matter what the cost."

"I believe you." It was almost like a vow.

He looked at her suddenly, and his face was very close to hers. Their hands, clasped atop Davis's picture, seemed to bind them together.

"We're going to do this, Annie. Don't doubt it."

His voice was very soft, but she had the sense she'd be able to hear him even if he just thought the words.

"I know."

He was so close that the slightest movement would bring his face against hers. For a second she thought he'd move, thought he'd lay his cheek close against hers and fold his arms around her. She didn't—she couldn't—

Then he was drawing back, closing the album, putting cool space between them. His head was turned away, and she couldn't see his expression.

Just as well. She leaned back, trying to still her chaotic thoughts. Link had shown her depths within himself, had touched her at a level she didn't want to expose. What had happened to the guard she kept around her emotions? What would happen if she let him get too close again?

Chapter Five

Leaving Marcy in the church nursery on Sunday morning had been harder than Annie had expected. She'd felt as if she were leaving part of herself behind, and the fact that Marcy had happily toddled over to the toy box hadn't really helped. She still hadn't wanted to leave her.

Overprotective? Probably.

Annie sat erect in the pew next to Link. She tried to concentrate on the Psalm reading, tried not to feel as if every person in the sanctuary watched them, but her effort was useless. The back of her neck prickled with the effect of those stares.

Naturally people were curious. Lakeview was a small town, where everyone knew everyone else. When two prominent citizens died and a custody battle started over their young child, people would wonder, especially when they heard about her sudden marriage to Link.

Frank and Julia were members here, although Becca had said they seldom attended. Still, that might be another reason why the Lesters would garner support.

She glanced at Link, sitting quietly next to her in the heavy walnut pew where Davis's family had sat for generations. Everything about the church—the stone exterior in the same style and material as the courthouse, the massive pews and pulpit, the soaring Gothic arches—proclaimed that this church had served the people of God in this place for a hundred years and would do so for a hundred more. Even the stained-glass windows with their memorial plaques for congregants long dead announced stability and tradition, reminding her that she didn't belong in Lakeview.

If Link felt out of place or disliked the stares of the congregation, it didn't show. He looked up at the rose window above the pulpit, apparently listening intently as the choir began the anthem. He seemed as distant from her now as he'd been since the night they'd looked at the photo albums together, the night she'd thought he was going to kiss her.

Since that night he'd put in long hours at the site and the office, then come home and closeted himself in Davis's small study. Had he been avoiding her or just stressed with work? She wasn't sure. The trouble was that avoiding her meant that he avoided Marcy, too.

She gave him another sidelong glance. What lay hidden by that square, determined jaw and firm mouth? Link had revealed something of himself when they'd looked at those pictures of Davis's family. Maybe he'd been regretting that ever since. He wasn't a person to give away his feelings, any more than she was.

The choir finished on a chord that vibrated to the arched ceiling, and sat in a rustle of robes. Garth stepped to the pulpit, grasping its sides the way he had the day he'd spoken at Davis and Becca's funeral.

Next to her, she saw Link's hands clasp each other until the knuckles whitened. She glanced at her own and saw that they looked exactly the same. The common grief she and Link shared had created an intimacy between them that she didn't know quite how to handle.

Garth read the second scripture passage—the story of Samuel's anointing of the boy David to be king of Israel. God had passed over the older, taller, stronger sons of Jesse until Samuel reached the boy.

Man looks on the outward appearance, but God looks on the heart.

At this moment, God could see into Link's heart far better than she could. He understood the grief they shared, saw the feelings that drove Link.

Father, you know how worried I am about this sit-

uation. I keep feeling my way, afraid each step will be a mistake. Please, guide me.

The words Link had spoken floated up to the surface of her mind. *I love Marcy for Davis's sake. I'll protect her inheritance no matter what.*

That was what troubled her. She suddenly saw it as clearly as if God had printed it out in large letters for her to read. Link was focused on preserving Marcy's inheritance, rather than on loving Marcy. That was why she couldn't quite bring herself to trust him.

She looked up at Garth, realizing she'd been so intent that she'd missed part of his sermon. But maybe God had opened her mind to what she really needed to hear.

By the time the final *Amen* was said, Annie knew what she had to do. She had to help Link love Marcy for herself alone. If he did, she could stop fearing that he'd do the wrong thing out of his zealous determination to save the company for the child at all costs.

The only question was, how could she bring that about?

She followed Link out of the pew. Nora Evers, fluttering in a black-and-white dress that matched her black-and-white hat, caught her arm as she moved into the aisle.

"Don't forget about the Bible study tonight." Nora pressed her hand. "I'll stop for you at about quarter of seven."

Nora had invited her to the study group Garth led

on Sunday evenings. She hadn't actually said she'd go, but Nora seemed to assume it. She glanced at Link. If she went, he'd have to stay with Marcy. He wouldn't have any choice about getting to know her better.

"I'll be ready." She smiled at the older woman. "I'm sure Link won't mind."

Link eyed her as Nora moved off. "What is it Link won't mind?"

"Watching Marcy tonight while I attend Garth's Bible study class."

He frowned. "I have a lot of work to do. Can't you get someone else?"

"Who? Nora's the only one I'd feel comfortable leaving her with, and Nora's going to the study."

Link glanced around, as if making sure no one in the throng moving out the aisle was paying attention to their conversation. "Look, I've got to leave work early tomorrow as it is for the social worker's visit."

"I'm sure the social worker will be impressed when she learns you're comfortable enough with Marcy to take care of her alone."

His eyes narrowed, as if he prepared another argument. Before he could speak, a small figure hurtled into his legs and bounced back.

"Stop that, Jeremy." A slight woman who didn't look old enough to be the child's mother grabbed him.

The woman straightened, pushing a strand of auburn hair away from her face, and Annie recognized her. One of Becca's close friends, but which one? Names rattled through her mind.

"Jenna Elliot," the woman said quickly. "I'm sure you don't remember me—"

"Of course I do. You brought dinner over the night I arrived." The wheels had begun to turn now. Becca and Jenna had started a play group together for their toddlers.

Jenna nodded, ignoring the way the four-year-old tugged at her hand. "I've got to pick up the baby from the nursery, but I just wanted to remind you of play group at my house this week."

"Well, I—"

"I'll call you." Jenna let the little boy pull her down the aisle. "See you Wednesday."

She worried at it as Link piloted her to the side door that led into the church's education wing. She ought to be happy to participate in the play group. She wasn't.

Link stopped next to a bulletin board decorated with Noah, the ark and a variety of colorful animals that had obviously been created by small hands. The corridor was empty, although voices echoed from the nursery. He looked down at her, a question in his dark eyes.

"Why don't you want to attend the play group?"

Could he read her mind? "What makes you think I don't want to?"

Link's straight brows lifted. "Do you?"

She concentrated on a zebra whose stripes were,

for some reason, red and green. "I guess I should go. It would be good for Marcy."

"But you don't want to. Why?" He propped his shoulder against the bulletin board, plainly prepared to stay there all day until she answered.

"It makes me uncomfortable." The words came out reluctantly. "It feels like I'm trying to take Becca's place." Tears suddenly stung her eyes.

Link gripped her hand in quick, wordless sympathy. "You are taking her place, Annie. But it's not as if you chose this."

She blinked rapidly to hold back the tears. "I just—" How could she explain something she didn't understand herself?

"They were Becca's closest friends. They'll want to be your friends, too."

That had a familiar echo. Becca had made friends so easily. People couldn't help responding to her warmth and joy. She'd always moved into friendship more cautiously, feeling more comfortable being the onlooker.

"Tell you what." Link's grasp tightened, compelling her attention.

She looked up, to find him half smiling. "What?"

"I'll put my doubts aside and take care of Marcy tonight. You put yours aside and go to play group on Wednesday. Deal?"

Apparently God wasn't the only one who could see into her heart.

"All right," she said reluctantly. "It's a deal."

* * *

How had he gotten himself into this? Link tried to keep Marcy from wiggling off the changing table while he put her into her pajamas.

That process was a lot easier said than done. He'd get one foot in, and while he was putting the other one in, the first one would pop out.

"Come on, honey, give me a break!"

For some reason, Marcy seemed to find that funny. She giggled, grabbing at his face, and he quickly pulled the pajamas up.

"Okay, we're going to get this done." He'd noticed that Annie always talked to the child while she was doing something. Maybe that was the solution.

Marcy looked up at him while he snapped the pajamas, her blue eyes wide and round. "Nan?"

"Nan had to go out for a while." Had she? Or had that been an excuse to get him involved with the baby? "She'll be back in a little bit. Link will put you to bed."

Marcy looked doubtful. Well, no more doubtful than he felt.

He'd jumped into baby-sitting impulsively, driven partly by his sense of obligation and partly by his desire to see Annie do something he thought would improve their chances with the social worker.

It hadn't taken much thought to decide Annie ought to belong to the play group. All he'd had to do was question whether his mother ever would have done such a thing.

Of course not. So the answer was that a good mother would do exactly the opposite of what his had done.

He picked Marcy up, and the child settled comfortably in his arms. Annie's hesitation had hinted at a shyness behind her cool composure. He hadn't guessed at that. Still, she'd be fine. Jenna and the other women had been Becca's friends. They'd make her feel welcome for Becca's sake.

"Okay, sweetie, time for bed." He swung the baby over the crib railing as he'd done once before. She clung to him, letting out a cry that nearly pierced his eardrums.

"Hey, what's wrong? You always go right down for Link and Nan, remember?"

Apparently not. Marcy wrapped small arms around his neck and held on tight.

He patted her back. "Come on, sweetie. Link has work to do. Be a good girl and go to bed. I'll sing you a song."

That didn't work. Neither did three stories in a row or four more lullabies.

He tried plopping her in the crib and making a hasty retreat. In the hallway, he leaned against the wall. He discovered that his tolerance for heart-rending cries was only about a minute and a half.

He pushed open the door and switched on the light. "Okay. I guess we're just not ready to go to bed yet."

He gave a fleeting thought to the work he'd expected to get through tonight—the record-keeping he'd taken for granted when Davis was doing it. Well, Annie shouldn't be too late. He hoped.

An hour later he and Marcy were still on the family room floor. He'd build a tower with blocks, she'd knock it over. Simple way of keeping her entertained, except that she was so tired she lay on the rug, reaching out with one chubby hand to knock the tower down.

He heard Annie's key in the lock with a mix of relief and annoyance.

"Why on earth is she still up?" Annie put her Bible and a notebook on the side table and slid her jacket off. She knelt beside Marcy. "What are you doing, sweetpea?"

"Mostly she's been crying every time I try to put her in bed."

Annie pulled the baby onto her lap. Marcy snuggled against Annie's soft yellow sweater. He shouldn't be noticing that the color brought out unexpected gold highlights in Annie's brown eyes. She dropped a kiss on the baby's curls, then looked at him, brows lifting.

"Did you try singing to her?"

"Every lullaby I know. And I read her favorite stories. Nothing doing."

He hated the defensive note in his voice. Why should he be defensive? This wasn't part of their deal. He was supposed to take care of the company, not the baby.

Annie stroked Marcy's back. The baby's eyes closed. "Did you try patting her?"

"I tried everything. She was fine until I put her in the crib, and then she'd scream as if I were deserting her."

Deserting her. His father had taken off as soon as he'd learned Link's mother was pregnant. If you needed a role model in order to be a decent father, he was out of luck.

"Well, let's give it another try." Annie started to rise, holding the baby, and he caught her elbow to help her up. The yellow sweater was as soft as it looked, and her hair swung against his arm like dark silk.

Okay, he definitely shouldn't be thinking things like that about Annie. He shouldn't be thinking about Annie at all. This was a business partnership. He took care of the construction company, and she took care of the baby. They would be safer if they didn't mix the two.

He let her go, and she took a step away, then looked at him questioningly.

"Aren't you coming up with us?"

"You'll do better without me. I've got work to do. I have a company to run, remember?"

Annie's mouth seemed to tighten, as if he'd said the wrong thing.

"Just don't forget that we have a meeting with the social worker tomorrow." She turned toward the stairs.

They'll take you away and put you in a home. He hadn't heard his mother's voice in years, but now it echoed in his head.

"Is it really that important for me to be here? Doesn't she just have to check out the house?"

Annie spun around, dark hair swinging against her cheeks. Marcy was already asleep on her shoulder.

"Of course it's important." Her voice was as sharp as he'd ever heard it. "That's the whole point, remember? We have to convince her that we're a family, that we can make a home for Marcy."

They'll take you away—

He clamped the door shut on that memory, but it kept sliding through the cracks. How did someone who'd never known a home figure out how to create one? He could build a house, but that wasn't the same thing.

Still, he didn't have a choice about this, and he knew it. Davis had trusted him. Annie was counting on him.

"Right." He took a breath, pasted a smile on his face. "I'll be here."

"Oh, Marcy, don't do that." Annie raced across the family room. While she'd been in the kitchen, dithering about whether or not she should offer coffee to the social worker, Marcy had been quietly pulling all the video tapes out of their cases.

"Here, honey, play with your nice teddy."

Marcy threw the teddy bear across the floor and

dived toward the videotapes again as the door swung open. Annie's heart nearly stopped, until she realized it was Link.

"Planning a video show?" He dropped his jacket on the nearest chair.

Annie scooped up the baby and handed her to Link. "Please, take her. And hang up your jacket. We've got to have things cleaned up by the time that woman gets here."

His eyebrows rose at her tone, but he took Marcy and picked up his jacket again.

She shouldn't be taking her tension out on him, but she'd been worried, ever since his comment the previous night, that he wouldn't show up on time.

"It'll be okay." He came back from the closet, lifting Marcy to his shoulders. "I'm sure she doesn't expect a house with a baby to be spotless all the time." He sounded as if he was trying to convince himself.

"I wish I believed that." She shoved the last videotape into place and glanced around the kitchen and family room, hands on her hips. "Since we spend most of our time in here, I thought we'd talk here instead of the living room. Should I offer her coffee? Does that pine air freshener smell all right, or did I overdo it?"

"I think you should calm down." He plopped Marcy into her toy car and steered her across the family room, making her laugh. "It's going to be okay."

Usually Marcy's laugh made him smile. At the moment, his mouth was tight. In spite of his words, he looked as nervous about this visit as she felt, maybe more so.

"Right." She took a deep breath and sent up a silent prayer for guidance. "We'll be okay."

The doorbell rang as soon as the words were out of her mouth. Her stomach seemed to turn over, and Link stiffened.

Okay, she thought. *Oh, Becca, I wish you were here.*

She opened the door. "Please, won't you come in?"

The woman—Mrs. Enid Bradshaw—looked as if she were in her mid-fifties, pleasant and grandmotherly until you noticed how shrewd her blue eyes were behind her gold-rimmed glasses.

"Mrs. Morgan, I'm happy to meet you." She shook hands, then stepped past Annie into the family room, focusing in on Link. She held out her hand. "And Mr. Morgan."

Link shook hands, nodding curtly. Annie frowned at him behind the woman's back. He ought to be a little more forthcoming than that.

"Won't you sit down? And would you care for some coffee?" She clasped her hands behind her back, sure that if she gestured with them, she'd knock something over.

"No coffee for me, thanks." The woman settled onto the couch and patted the cushion next to her. "Let's sit down and get acquainted."

Annie obediently sat next to her, then glanced at Link. He didn't make any move to come over to them, but continued to rock the baby back and forth in her car.

Mrs. Bradshaw beamed at Marcy. "Such a big girl. I guess she likes her car, doesn't she."

"Especially when she can get Link to push her around the house." She frowned at Link. Why was he just standing there? She took a deep breath. Maybe she ought to plunge right in. "Why don't you tell us what you need to know, Mrs. Bradshaw. We'll try to answer any questions you have."

The woman's gaze moved from Annie to Link to the baby. "I'm sure you're feeling nervous about this whole situation, so I'll tell you what I have in mind. I'd like for us to talk a bit, about how you're doing and how Marcy's doing. Then perhaps you'd show me around the house." She smiled. "I promise, I won't look in any closets. Doesn't sound too bad, does it?"

"No." She tried to smile, tried to tell herself that the woman just wanted what was best for Marcy. That surely, if Mrs. Bradshaw was good at her job, she'd see how much Annie loved the baby.

"Let's start with how the two of you are doing. This has been a difficult time for both of you, hasn't it?"

For an instant she thought the lump in her throat would keep her from speaking. She had to force the words out. "We both lost people who were very dear to us. I'm not sure I've taken it in yet," she said as her gaze brushed the family photo on the bookcase.

"And of course it's a big life change for a career woman like yourself."

That sounded like a direct quote from Frank Lester. Had Mrs. Bradshaw met with them already? She didn't dare ask. Or maybe it was just that her inexperience as a mother was written all over her face.

"My niece means everything to me." She met the woman's gaze squarely. "I'd give up any job for her."

The woman nodded, then glanced at Link. He'd sat down on the rug with Marcy in his lap, and they both seemed intent on the jack-in-the-box he'd taken out of the cabinet where Marcy's toys were stored. All Link's focus was on the baby. Worry pricked her. Would the social worker think it odd he was not participating in the conversation more?

"What about you, Mr. Morgan? How are you getting along?"

"All right."

Annie frowned at him. He blinked, then seemed to realize something more was expected of him.

"Davis had been my best friend since college. I miss him. But it helps that I can do something for his child."

"This hasn't been the best way to start out married life, has it."

If she waited for Link to answer that one, Annie suspected, she'd be waiting a long time. His explanations of why this marriage was best for all of them seemed to have deserted him.

"We're both dealing with our grief and the changes in our lives. But Link and I have known each other for a long time, so that makes things easier." She wasn't going to lie to the woman, implying that this had been some grand, romantic love match. "We both love Marcy and want what's best for her. We believe that's what our marriage gives her."

"Do you have anything to add, Mr. Morgan?"

For a moment she thought he wouldn't answer at all, and her nerves tightened to the breaking point. Finally he shook his head.

"I think Annie has put it very well."

"Fine." Mrs. Bradshaw put both hands on her knees and stood up quickly. "Why don't you show me the rest of the house, then?"

"But—" She stood up automatically. "Don't you want to ask us anything else?" *We've blown it. She thinks we're so terrible she's not even going to bother asking the rest of her questions.*

"There'll be plenty of time for that." She smiled, but Annie couldn't read the expression in those shrewd eyes. "We'll be visiting together a number of times."

We've blown it. We really have.

She couldn't stop the refrain from repeating itself in her mind as she led the social worker through the house. The woman had said she wouldn't look in any closets, but she did check under the sink in the kitchen and in each bathroom, as if to be sure they hadn't left anything dangerous there.

They paused in the nursery, Mrs. Bradshaw looking around in appreciation. ''This is charming.''

''My sister designed it herself.'' Her throat was tight again. ''I came down one weekend and helped her put up the wallpaper border. She was so happy with how it turned out.''

Nodding, the woman went back into the hall, peeking into the master bedroom and bath, then the guest room and Davis's small office, strewn now with the papers and blueprints Link had brought in.

Had she noticed the obvious signs that Annie and Link were not sharing a bedroom? Annie held her breath, waiting for the woman to ask about it, but she didn't.

They trooped back downstairs. Link still didn't say anything, and Annie's frustration mounted. Couldn't he even try to be pleasant to the woman?

Mrs. Bradshaw shook hands with both of them, tickled Marcy's soft cheek and made her way out of the family room. The door closed behind her.

Annie stood at the family room window, a smile frozen on her face, until the social worker's car had disappeared down the street. Then she swung toward Link.

''What on earth is wrong? You barely spoke to the woman the whole time she was here. Are you trying to make us lose Marcy?''

Chapter Six

Link stared at Annie, her question echoing between them.

His head throbbed in time with the blocks Marcy was pounding. He could hardly think, let alone speak. *Careful. Don't lose it. Don't let her know the truth.*

"What are you talking about? Mrs. Bradshaw seemed friendly enough. I thought it went well." He leaned against the back of the lounge chair with forced casualness and tried to sound as if he actually believed that.

"Went well?" Annie stood framed by the door for a moment, the light from its window behind her. Then she took a quick step toward him. "How can you say that?"

He shrugged, still so tense that the movement of his shoulders felt stiff. "She didn't ask any hard questions. You were able to cope with everything."

If I said too much, I was afraid she'd see right through me. Social workers probably develop a gift for that.

"Yes, *I* did." Annie planted her hands on her hips. By the look in her eyes, he suspected she'd rather use them to throttle him.

"Look, I answered every question the woman asked me." He straightened, knowing he couldn't hold a casual pose any longer. The things he couldn't say kept beating in his mind. "Men don't talk about their feelings. If she's any kind of a social worker, she must know that."

Annie shook her head, her mouth set. "That's a pretty feeble excuse."

Marcy stopped pounding with her blocks and looked up at him as if she agreed.

"It's the only one you'll get." His anger flared. "I'm going out."

He started to move past Annie toward the door. She grabbed his wrist.

"You've got to tell me what's going on, Link. We have an agreement. This situation is too important for either of us to let our feelings get in the way."

He could pull free of her in an instant. He didn't want to.

Her fingers tightened against his skin, demanding an answer. "Tell me."

He did jerk free then, but he didn't go out the door. He couldn't.

Annie was right. He'd gotten them into this, and

the least he owed her was as much of the truth as he could manage to say.

"All right!" He turned away, not wanting to look at her, and found himself facing the photo of Davis on the bookshelf. His friend looked back at him. With reproach? He wasn't sure what Davis would think of this. They'd both had secrets to hide.

"All right," he said again, more quietly. "I'm sorry. I didn't realize it would bother me so much to have the social worker looking into our situation. I thought I could handle it."

"But you couldn't." Annie's voice had gone soft, too, as if she knew this was important. "Why, Link? What have you ever had to do with social workers?"

He swung toward her, feeling his lips twist when he tried to smile. "You never knew about my background, did you?" He made the thing he'd always feared into a question. "Davis didn't tell Becca, Becca didn't repeat it to you?"

"I don't know what Davis might have told Becca, but I've never known anything about your life before you became Davis's roommate." Her gaze was very steady, assuring him that she was telling the truth.

Not that he could doubt it. Annie didn't lie.

He had to do something, not just watch her face while he said this. He planted both hands against the bookcase, as if he intended to push it right through the wall.

"Let's just say I didn't have the kind of family background Davis did, with the nice house and the name in the community and the secure position going back generations in the same place.''

He felt her move closer, but she didn't attempt to touch him.

''Neither did Becca and I, for that matter. We weren't like the Conrads of Lakeview. We were just ordinary, middle-class people. That doesn't make me afraid of social workers.''

''I'm not afraid!''

Liar. You're afraid she's going to turn you back into that kid again—the one nobody wanted.

''What would you call it, then?''

He stopped trying to push the bookcase through the wall and straightened. ''Okay. Maybe *afraid* isn't a bad word for it. You might be, too, if you'd grown up like I did.''

''What—''

He swung toward her before she could ask the question. ''My mother was a drunk, is that plain enough? I never knew my father—he had sense enough to beat it before I was born. It wasn't exactly the perfect childhood.''

''Mrs. Bradshaw reminded you.''

If that was pity in her voice, he didn't want it. ''My mother always said that if I didn't behave, the social worker would put me in a home. She used that as a reason to stay on the move from town to town, always starting over, always looking for something we didn't have.'' His stomach twisted with the effort to suppress the kid he'd been. "The only place she ever found what she wanted was in a bottle."

"Link, I'm sorry." Annie's voice broke, and she reached out to touch him.

He jerked away from her hand. "I don't want your pity. I just want you to understand."

"All right. No pity." Her brown eyes were bright with tears, and she took an audible breath as if to steady herself. "Just facts. We have to look like a family to Mrs. Bradshaw, no matter what our feelings are."

Look like a family. He hadn't realized how hard that would be, or he wouldn't have gotten them into this.

No, that was wrong. He would have, because this was the only way to save the company.

"Look, nothing in my life ever prepared me to be a father. I don't know how to be what I've never experienced, and nothing you say will change that."

Her mouth trembled but she didn't speak. That just made him feel worse.

"I'll save the company for Marcy if I can." He grabbed his jacket, knowing he had to get out of there. "That's the best I can do, and it'll have to be enough."

Annie had spent twenty-four hours thinking and praying, and she still didn't know what to make of Link's revelation. Every time she tried to think rationally about his childhood, she was overwhelmed with a mixture of pity and fear.

She maneuvered the stroller over the curb at the corner of the square, heading toward the Town House Restaurant to meet Link for dinner. The afternoon had turned windy, so she'd dressed Marcy in her bright red fleecy jacket with the hood. The baby's blond hair curled around the edge of the hood as she leaned forward to bat the fabric blocks that were linked to the stroller frame.

Link had barely spoken since he'd stormed out of the house the night before. Stormed? Or fled? He'd certainly been trying to escape. He'd been embarrassed either about exposing his secret or about the pity she'd been unwise enough to show.

He hadn't come back to the house until after she'd gone to bed. She'd heard his careful steps in the hall as he'd tiptoed past the baby's room, had listened to the sound of the guest room door close.

Had he slept at all? She didn't know. Her sleep had certainly been troubled, to say the least. She'd finally fallen into a deep slumber around dawn, and Link had been gone when she woke.

He'd called later, suggesting she and Marcy meet him at the Town House for supper. He'd sounded perfectly normal, as if yesterday's emotions were just a dream.

If that was how he wanted to play this, she'd have no choice but to go along with him. She glanced down at the gold ring on her left hand. Marriage apparently didn't give her the right to extend sympathy to him.

She kept being swamped with pity for the boy he'd been. Her imagination could easily fill in the blanks in his brief recital. He'd been an outsider—unloved and unwanted probably all his life until Davis had brought him to Lakeview.

Now he belonged here. She'd thought his determination to hold on to control of the company was almost too intense. Now she knew why. Conrad and Morgan wasn't just a company to him. It was his place in the world. What would he sacrifice to keep it?

She'd allowed herself to believe that she and Link were in this together. That was a dangerous illusion.

She couldn't count on him. She couldn't count on anyone. She was in this alone, and she had to make that clear to both of them.

Be with me, Lord. She grasped the brass handle of the restaurant door and pulled, struggling to get the stroller through the opening. *Be with me, because I don't have anyone else.*

The rush of warm, scented air welcomed her to the restaurant, and a teenaged waiter sprang to hold the door and help her with the stroller.

"Mrs. Morgan, your table is ready." He smiled down at the baby. "Hey, Marcy, what's cooking?"

Marcy reached for him with an answering smile, and he tickled her cheek.

"Looks as if you're old friends."

"I'm Tommy Evers." The boy had a spattering of freckles to go with his red hair. "My gram is your next-door neighbor. Marcy knows me from church nursery, too."

Simple, wasn't it? She just wasn't used to the permutations of small-town life. And she couldn't let herself depend on that life, either. These people could be lining up solidly behind the Leators, for all she knew.

He pushed the stroller. "This way. We'll get you guys settled. Link hasn't come in yet."

He led her to a corner table and lifted Marcy to the high chair he had ready. "I'll be back in a sec with your menus."

The Town House was all dark-paneled walls, brass light fixtures and white tablecloths. Tuesday must be quiet—only three other tables were occupied. She was just taking the baby's jacket off when the outer door swung open again. Link had arrived.

The surge of pleasure she felt at the sight of his tall figure dismayed her. *You're in this alone,* she reminded herself. *Link has his own interests to protect.*

For the moment their interests coincided, but if that changed… She didn't want to finish that thought.

"Hi." Link responded to Marcy's pleased crow with a light kiss on the top of her head. He slid into the chair opposite Annie, his presence seeming to complete the circle around the table.

He must have changed at the office, since he hadn't come back to the house. He'd put on a cream-colored fisherman's sweater that made his dark hair gleam in contrast. And she shouldn't be noticing that.

The waiter returned at that moment. While he and Link analyzed the high school football team's chances at the upcoming game, she lectured herself into her usual common sense.

Once the waiter left with their orders, she tried to find something to talk about. "I take it you follow the local football team." That was an inane comment, but better than nothing.

"Sure." He looked surprised. "Everyone does."

She lifted an eyebrow. "Not in Boston."

"Okay, not in cities, I guess. In small towns, what else would you do on Friday nights?" He eyed her speculatively. "What do you usually do on a Friday night back in Boston?"

She shrugged, glancing down at her place mat. "Nothing very exciting, I suppose. I'm usually ready to collapse with a video after working all week. If I'm going out, I save that 'til Saturday. And Sundays I spend with my folks."

It probably sounded boring. It probably *was* boring, but it was real, unlike the fantasy they were trying to create here.

Before he could say something polite about her mundane life, a couple from another table stopped by. The man started talking to Link about the progress they'd made at the job that day. The woman looked at Annie with frank curiosity until Link introduced them.

"This is Linda and Joe Trent. Joe works with me, and Linda was a friend of Becca's."

"Actually, I'm in the play group Becca started." The petite brunette bent to plant a kiss on Marcy's cheek. "Hi, sweet baby. Charlie can't wait to see you at play group." She smiled at Annie. "My little guy's two, and he's got the biggest crush on Marcy—always trying to hug her. You're going to continue with play group, aren't you?"

Aware of Link's gaze on her, she nodded. "I hope to."

"I'll see you there, then. And if you need any help with anything..."

"Come on, honey, let them have their dinner in peace. You can talk tomorrow." Joe steered his wife away from the table. "See you."

Salads appeared in front of them, as if Tommy had been waiting until the others were out of the way. Link shook his white napkin and dropped it in his lap.

"Sorry about that."

"People are curious, I guess."

He nodded. "That's natural enough. Around here, you tend to see the same people everywhere you go. And everyone knew Davis and Becca. I'm surprised you haven't met Becca's play group friends when you were here visiting."

"Actually, I think Becca introduced some of them at one time or another. But I was here to visit Becca and her family, not to become part of the Lakeview community."

I didn't want to then. This was Becca's place, not mine. I don't belong here.

Link paused with a forkful of greens halfway to his mouth. "Things are different now. You need to be part of it."

"Just because it's important to you—" She stopped. That came dangerously close to bringing up the things he'd told her.

His face tightened. "I'm not talking about myself. I was thinking of the Lesters."

A shiver worked down her spine. She said the thing she feared. "You think the case might go their way because their family's been part of this community for generations."

His brow furrowed. "I hope that won't work against us." He met her gaze. "But I don't know. It sure wouldn't hurt to try and make some friends."

"I already said I'd go to the play group." She attacked her salad with her fork.

"You make it sound like a work gang. They're all nice people. They were—"

"Becca's friends. I know." They would be nice to her for Becca's sake. "We don't have similar interests. We won't have anything to talk about. But...I'm sure they all know more about raising babies than I do. Maybe I can pick up some pointers."

Link clasped her hand where it lay on the table between them. "We're going to win this. You'll see. We have to."

The warmth from his hand traveled right up her arm and into her heart.

No. She couldn't let herself feel that. She couldn't let herself start counting on Link, no matter how comforting that might be. Hadn't she just told herself that?

But she wanted to. She couldn't possibly deny that.

Link came back to the house warily the next afternoon. If the play group hadn't gone well, Annie would need help he didn't know how to give her. Emotions weren't his strong suit.

He paused inside the family room door, listening. Someone was playing "The Wheels on the Bus" on the piano in the living room.

It obviously couldn't be Marcy, so it must be Annie. He hadn't even known she played.

He dropped the things he was carrying on the sofa and went softly across to the archway. Annie played, and Marcy sat on the rug next to the piano bench, her chubby hands spinning wildly.

Marcy saw him first. "Wheels!" she shouted.

"I see wheels." He picked her up and swung her in the air. "Are you singing with Nan?"

Annie had stopped playing the moment she realized he was there. She pulled her hands from the keys and slid off the bench as if she'd been caught doing something wrong.

He grabbed her hand and tugged her toward the bench. "Don't stop now. I want to join the party."

"I don't play for people to hear. I'm not very good." She was actually blushing.

"Marcy's people. You were playing for her." Teasing Annie felt like old times.

"Marcy's twenty months old. She just likes the noise."

"So pretend I'm twenty months, too." He slid onto the piano bench, Marcy in his lap, and glanced up at her.

Annie stood, hesitating, her hands clasped behind her as if to deny their ability. The baby reached for the keys, and he clasped her arms and began rotating them in the motions of the song.

"Come on. Take it from the top."

Half smiling, she slid onto the bench next to him. "All right, but you'd better be as uncritical as Marcy is."

She started to play the song again, slowly at first, then gaining speed as the baby laughed and swung her hands in obvious pleasure. Link sang along, stumbling over the words as she stumbled over the keys now and then.

They did the last chorus, and he helped Marcy clap.

"Good job, little girl. I'll bet you sang that at play group today, didn't you?"

Marcy sputtered something incomprehensible, and he looked at Annie, knowing it was time to ask her how it went. He hadn't understood her hesitation— still didn't. What was so scary about a bunch of mommies and babies?

"We must have sung twenty songs. Who would guess that toddlers would know so many?" Annie looked at the piano keys, not at him, flexing her fingers as if she wanted to play some more.

"Did you play for them?"

She looked at him, eyes startled. "Goodness, no. I told you, I don't play for people." She touched the polished wood of the piano gently. "Marcy just had so much fun with the songs that I thought I'd try it when we got home."

He may as well ask. She probably wouldn't volunteer anything. "So, what about you? Did you have fun?"

Her lips twitched. "You want me to admit you were right, don't you?"

Relieved, he grinned. "I was, wasn't I?"

"They were all lovely to me. We watched the children play, had brunch, talked." She played a soft chord, then met his eyes. "We talked about Becca. I was ashamed of myself. I hadn't thought about how much they must be hurting, too."

He discovered his throat was tight. "I can guess. It's the little everyday things that catch you up—wanting to tell them something, then realizing they're not there."

"It's happening to you, too."

He nodded. "Davis was more than just a friend. We'd worked together for so long, it was almost like I knew what he thought before he said it. I feel like a piece of me is missing."

"I know." Her voice was soft. She studied the keys, her silky hair swinging down to hide her face. "That summer at the shore I could tell you were as close to each other as Becca and I were."

"Maybe that's why the four of us fit together so well."

"We did, didn't we?"

She tilted her face up, and he saw the hint of a smile.

"But Becca knew from the first moment what she wanted."

"Davis was about as bad."

Her smiled widened, as if it didn't hurt so much to think of the distant past as the recent past. "You only asked me out because Davis pushed you into it."

"That's not true." At her knowing look, he grinned. "Well, not entirely true. You intrigued me."

"Me?"

"Yes, you." He flicked her soft cheek with one finger. "You, with your serious look and that little frown you wore when you were afraid Becca might do something she shouldn't. I wanted to know why you were so serious."

"Comes of being the oldest."

She smiled, but a shadow crossed her eyes at the words, as if there was more to it than that. Suddenly he was right back to the kid he'd been then, determined to know what lay behind that cool reserve Annie wore like a shield. Wanting to know what she'd do if he kissed her.

His hand hovered near her cheek, and the longing to touch her was so strong it nearly made him forget where they were and why. Nearly, but not quite.

He put his hand down slowly, hoping she hadn't noticed. That was all they'd need to complicate matters beyond belief.

He'd hurt her once before, when he couldn't tell her the truth about Davis. They'd lost what might have been between them then, if the circumstances had been different.

He'd pushed her into this marriage. What kind of man would he be if he took advantage of the situation now?

Chapter Seven

Annie felt as if a wall had suddenly gone up between her and Link. They still sat side by side on the piano bench, the baby still babbled on Link's lap, but he had retreated behind an impenetrable shield.

She played a few chords at random, trying to regain her composure. She had to say something, anything, to get things back to a normal level. The longer this silence lasted, the worse it would be.

"Well, anyway, I'm glad I went to the play group today, and not just because of whatever Mrs. Bradshaw might think. Jenna invited me to take the babies for a walk tomorrow if it's sunny out."

"Jenna's a good person." He seemed to make an effort to bring himself back from wherever he'd been.

All right, this was better. No more awkward moments.

"I offered to host the next meeting here. Jenna said she'd help me."

He lifted an eyebrow. "You're really getting into a social whirl."

"You're the one who said I had to be a part of the community, remember?" She was glad to turn his words back on him.

"Hey, I'm happy about it. I'll even run the vacuum for you the night before."

"I'll hold you to that." She smiled. "By the way, we're bringing pictures of the parents when they were babies to the next meeting. One of the women is into making scrapbooks, and she's going to show us how to mat them. When I find Becca's baby pictures, I'll prove to you that Marcy looks like her."

Link stroked the baby's hair. "Okay, okay." His smile erased the last vestiges of strain from his face. "She's a beautiful little girl, wherever it came from."

"She is that." She touched Marcy's cheek gently, relaxing. Whatever had been wrong between her and Link was put right again. Now she just had to find some way of avoiding those emotional minefields.

"That reminds me." Link slid from the piano bench, putting Marcy down. "I brought something home I want to show you."

He headed for the family room, with Marcy toddling after him. Annie caught up with them as he picked up something from the sofa just before the baby's inquiring fingers reached it.

"Not for you, sweetheart."

"A camera."

He nodded. "I had this at the office. We use it to keep a record of the work we've done."

He lifted the camera, focusing on her through the viewfinder, and she put up her hand in an automatic protest.

"Don't take my picture. I'm a mess."

He shifted the focus to Marcy. "You look fine. But it's really Marcy I had in mind. Or rather, Marcy with us."

"I don't know what you mean."

"Looking at photo albums the other night made me think of it." He lowered the camera. "Every family takes pictures of the things they do, right?"

"I suppose." She hadn't thought about it, but of course Becca had albums full of everything they'd done with Marcy since the day she was born.

"That's what we've got to do. We've got to take pictures, lots of pictures."

She got it then. "To show the social worker."

"And the judge, if we get the chance. We want to prove that we're just like any other family with a toddler."

Marcy grabbed for the dangling camera strap, and let out a shriek when Link took it from her. Annie bent to pick her up.

"Well, there's lesson one about families with toddlers. Never let mealtime be late." She bounced Marcy. "How about a little snack for you while Nan gets supper on?"

Marcy stopped crying and reached toward the kitchen.

Link laughed. "She might not say much, but she gets her meaning across."

He followed them to the kitchen, and when Annie handed Marcy an animal cracker, the camera flashed in her eyes.

"Do you have to do that now?"

"No time like the present. I'm not the world's greatest photographer. I'll have to take a lot of shots to get some decent ones."

She pulled the casserole from the oven and the aroma of chicken and noodles filled the air. Link kept up a running commentary of things they might do and photograph. It was impossible not to get caught up in his enthusiasm.

This was the Link she'd known—filled with energy, driving straight toward any goal with a single-minded determination that wiped out every obstacle.

Well, that was good, wasn't it? At least for the moment their goals coincided.

"Okay, this is about ready." She used pot holders to transfer the casserole to the table, placing it well away from the high chair. "Will you put Marcy in her chair and get a bib on her?"

Link put the camera aside. He lifted Marcy into the seat, but she slapped impatiently at the bib, reaching toward the casserole.

"That's too hot, sweetie."

She let out a wail that cut off abruptly when Annie

broke a piece of roll and put it on the tray. Marcy looked up at Link, grinning triumphantly around the roll.

"You're a con artist, you are." He grinned, picking up the camera again. "Come on, Annie, move in close so I can get both of you."

She brushed at her hair. "I look a mess."

"You look pretty, just like you always do. And this isn't about you." He focused the camera. "Good job." The camera flashed.

Annie knew he didn't mean anything by it. He was just trying to get her to cooperate. Silly to let his words warm her, she thought as she spooned noodles and chicken into Marcy's bowl.

Marcy reached eagerly for the bowl. Before Annie could get the spoon, she put her fist into the dish and stuffed a handful into her mouth, then grinned again.

Link started to laugh. "Her table manners aren't the greatest, but she knows what she wants."

Marcy chortled as if she'd meant to make him laugh, and Annie couldn't help smiling at the sound. Anyone looking at them would think they were a real family.

She was still smiling when the telephone rang, and she reached out to answer it.

"Mrs. Morgan?" Mrs. Bradshaw sounded as if she was in a hurry. "Sorry to call you so late. I wanted to let you know that I've tentatively set up a visit for Marcy with the Lesters for tomorrow morning. Can you have her there at nine o'clock?"

A chasm opened in front of her, and the happy family she'd been imagining vanished.

Link picked up the car keys and glanced at the clock. Eight-fifty. The breakfast he'd forced down felt like lead in his stomach, and this had to be far worse for Annie.

She came toward him across the family room, carrying Marcy. She'd dressed the baby in that little fuzzy red thing that made her look like one of Santa's elves. Compared to that, Annie's face was as white as a sheet of paper.

"Ready?" He gripped the keys and tried to think of something reassuring to say. He couldn't come up with anything that wouldn't sound trite.

Annie nodded, her mouth set. "I guess we'd better go. We don't want to be late."

"I don't care if we keep Frank and Julia waiting." He opened the door. "But we don't want to make the wrong impression on Mrs. Bradshaw."

"If she thinks I don't want to leave Marcy there, it'll be the truth." Annie went out, then waited while he locked the door.

He reached for Marcy. "Let me take her."

"No." She half turned away from him, arms circling the baby. "I've got her."

She'd been tense since that call from Mrs. Bradshaw. He'd heard her get up twice in the night, heard her soft footsteps cross the hall as she opened the nursery door and peeked in at Marcy.

Well, she wasn't likely to relax until this was over. Good thing he'd insisted that he'd go in to work late today so that he could drive them back and forth. He didn't want Annie driving this morning.

He waited while she put Marcy in her car seat, then held the door for her to get in the front. He paused for a moment before closing it, looking down at her. She'd buttoned a caramel-colored jacket against the morning air, but she still looked pinched.

"We knew this was coming." Stupid thing to say. Why would that make her feel any better? "It's just a visit."

"I know." She glanced at her watch. "We should go."

He went around, slid into his seat and started the car. Nothing he said was going to make this better, because nothing he said could make a difference. The Lesters would have their observed visit, like it or not.

Still, he had to try. "Believe me, I've been in the Lesters' house. It's not suited to a baby. That's the first thing Mrs. Bradshaw will see."

Anne showed a flicker of interest. "What's it like?"

"White carpets, glass tables, tile floors, expensive knickknacks all over the place." He shrugged. "Definitely not baby-proofed."

A crease formed between her brows. "I hope they'll keep a close eye on her. She's so fast."

Great, now he'd given her something else to worry about.

"They'll be at their most careful. After all, Mrs. Bradshaw will be there, watching them."

Annie glanced back toward Marcy. "This is one time when I wish she weren't quite so outgoing. She'll smile at anyone, whether she knows them or not."

"It won't make a difference." He tried to sound sure. "Julia's about as maternal as— well, I don't know what. But a baby is the last thing on her wish list."

Annie stirred, a little color coming into her face. "Becca told me that when she announced that she and Davis were having a baby, Julia acted sorry for her. Julia said she never wanted to have a child because they were too much trouble."

"That sounds like Julia. She's so obsessed with the latest fashions. I can't imagine she would be willing to risk losing her figure." He reached across the seat and squeezed her hand. It felt like ice. "You'll see. Mrs. Bradshaw will take one look at that place and see the truth."

"I hope you're right." It sounded like a prayer.

He pulled into the driveway. The Lester house, all glass and angles, sat on a hill overlooking the lake. Naturally Frank hadn't had them design his home.

He stopped at the front door. By the time he rounded the car, Annie was already lifting Marcy from the car seat.

He put his arm around both of them. "It'll be okay," he said softly. "Don't worry too much."

Annie nodded. For an instant she looked lost. Then

she settled Marcy in her arms and marched toward the door.

It opened before they could knock. Julia reached for Marcy with every indication of eagerness.

"There now, darling. Come to Aunt Julia."

He could feel the effort it took Annie to let go of the baby. She hesitated in the doorway, as if unwilling to turn away and leave.

Frank appeared behind his wife, smiling. "Julia, where are your manners? Invite Mr. and Mrs. Morgan in." He laid the faintest stress on the titles, as if mocking them.

Julia stepped back, gesturing them inside. He had no desire to enter Frank's house, but beyond them he could see Mrs. Bradshaw. It certainly couldn't hurt to gain a few more minutes with her, especially after the mess he'd made of her visit to them.

He grasped Annie's elbow in mute support and followed her into the house.

Frank rubbed his hands together. "Well, this is nice, having our favorite little girl in our house at last. We were just going to show Marcy's room to Mrs. Bradshaw. Maybe you'd like to see it, too."

Marcy's room? What was Frank trying to pull? Marcy had never even been in their house, which spoke volumes for how interested they'd been in her.

"Yes, do come along." Julia clutched Marcy tightly, as if fearing the child would try to get away. "We want you to see it."

They followed Julia across the wide living room. Light poured in from the floor-to-ceiling windows overlooking the lake, glittering off glass and metal tables and tile floors.

Julia led the way down a hall lined with mirrored closets and flung open a door. "There, you see. It's all ready for her."

He blinked. This had been a guest room where they'd left coats the one time he'd been to the Lester house. Now it had been transformed.

Pale aqua-and-white baby furniture, billowing white curtains, a pale aqua rug. Low shelves lined the walls, filled with more toys than the local toy store had in stock. The far wall and the ceiling were covered with an elaborate fairy-tale mural.

"Pink is so passé, don't you think?" Julia smiled possessively at the room. "This is much more elegant." She put Marcy down and began to unzip her jacket.

"Yes. Elegant." Annie's voice sounded strangled.

He wrapped his hand around hers, trying vainly to warm it. He'd told Annie that the social worker would take one look and see how unsuitable this place was for a child. He'd assured her it would be all right.

Which only went to show how little he knew. He gripped Annie's fingers tightly, and she clung to him. He'd underestimated Frank. He wouldn't make that mistake again.

Annie stared out the car window at the houses they passed. She took a breath, feeling as if it was the first time she'd done so since they'd left the Lesters.

She had to clear her throat before she could speak. "Where are we going?"

"I have to go to my apartment to pick up some papers I need." She felt Link's worried gaze touch her face. "Then I thought we could stop at the work site. After that, it'll be time to pick up Marcy."

"What if she doesn't want to leave?" She had a sudden, horrifying vision of Marcy crying at the thought of being torn away from all those toys. "What if—"

"You're overreacting, aren't you?" Link's tone was deliberately dampening.

She rubbed her forehead, trying vainly to massage away the tension. "Am I? Mrs. Bradshaw just saw a decorator's dream nursery."

"I have to hand it to Frank. He worked fast."

"Is that all you can say?" She felt a spurt of anger.

Link pulled into the parking lot in front of a block of apartments. He parked, then turned to her.

"Look, Annie, we knew Frank and Julia would cause problems. I have to admit, I didn't foresee that they'd set up a nursery to impress the social worker."

"But they did. Enid Bradshaw may think they've been longing to have a child."

"She's a smart cookie. She'll realize that 'Marcy's room' has been put together in the past week, and by a decorator, not by Julia. As for those toys, they probably went online and ordered everything that was recommended for a twenty-month-old."

"However they did it, they did a good job. I hope you're right about Mrs. Bradshaw, because I found it pretty impressive."

Link shook his head, then reached for the door handle. "Let's finish this conversation inside, okay?"

She followed him to the apartment door, then inside, stepping over a pile of mail that had been shoved through the mail slot. Link pushed envelopes and magazines out of the way, shut the door and turned to face her.

"Okay, what's this really about?"

"That should be obvious." She folded her arms across her chest. His apartment felt chilled and deserted. "The Lesters are—"

"The Lesters are two people interested in nothing more than Marcy's inheritance. I still say you're over-reacting." He frowned, looking at her searchingly.

"That's what we keep saying, isn't it." She rubbed her arms, turning away from Link's intense gaze. "But what if we're wrong?"

"What are you talking about?" Link caught her elbows and swung her around to face him. "Wrong about what?"

The insidious doubt that crept through her in the dark moments of the night suddenly blossomed. "What if I'm wrong? What if I'm not the best person for Marcy? I want to be, but—"

Link gave her a light shake. "Annie, wake up. You're letting fear get the better of you." He sounded angry. "This is Marcy we're talking about. You love that baby more than anyone else in the world. No one could be better for that child than you.''

His emotion pierced the misery that had surrounded her since she'd seen that picture-perfect nursery. She took a breath, forcing tight muscles to relax. She shook her head, smiling a little.

''You're right.''

His grip eased, but he still watched her warily. ''I'm glad you realize that.''

''I don't know what got into me. I just lost my confidence all of a sudden.''

''Well, don't. You're what's best for Marcy, and we're going to prove it. Right?''

She nodded. ''Right.''

''Okay, then.'' He released her. ''If you don't mind waiting a second, I'll get some things I need from the bedroom.''

He crossed the room with quick strides and disappeared through a doorway. She glanced around.

Becca had been right. The place did look like a motel. The beige carpeting and beige walls were typical of a rental unit, but most people would make the place their own with furnishings, pictures, knick-knacks.

It didn't look as if Link had done a thing. The faux-Danish-modern living room set had to have come with the apartment. Link surely wouldn't have gone out and bought it deliberately. The only personal item in sight was a photo of Link and Davis, wearing hard hats, standing in front of an excavation and grinning proudly.

Link had said he didn't know how to be a father. Based on the evidence, he also didn't know how to make a home. The neglected child who'd been hauled from one furnished apartment to another probably hadn't had a chance to learn that.

He came back into the room carrying a cardboard box, then picked up the photograph and added it to the contents. He glanced around, as if to see whether there was anything else worth taking.

"Not much of a home, is it?" he said.

His words echoed her thoughts so accurately that she couldn't deny them. "I guess you didn't spend a lot of time here."

"No." Perhaps he saw the apartment through her eyes. "Becca offered to help me fix it up, but there always seemed to be more important things to do." He shrugged, dismissing it. "Let's go."

He scooped his mail into the box and they went out, snapping the door shut on the empty rooms. She waited while he stowed the box in the trunk, shivering a little as the wind whipped fallen leaves across the parking lot. She'd been cold since she left the house that morning, and it wasn't just a question of the temperature.

The Lesters' place, elegant though it had been, hadn't felt like a home to her. The chill in the atmosphere hadn't been physical, but she'd felt it. They lived in an expensively decorated vacuum that didn't betray a thing about who they were or what they valued.

Link's apartment, cold and barren, spoke volumes about who he was. He was a man on the way up, too busy to be bothered with mundane things like home and family.

She was living in her sister's house, trying to pretend she was making a home there with Link. None of them had a real home. It was all pretend.

Chapter Eight

❧

"I have to speak to the men for a minute. You can stay here, if you want, so you won't get your shoes muddy. I'll be finished in plenty of time to pick up Marcy."

Annie nodded, then watched as Link strode quickly toward the bare frames of houses at the lakeside project. This was where Link's heart was—not in relationships or family. In his work. Specifically, in this project he and Davis had started.

She tried to visualize what Link saw in the clutter of raw framing, stacks of materials and piles of earth. He was building the houses into the hillside, facing the lake. The workers hadn't cut the surrounding trees, and the leaves that had begun to drift to the ground softened the raw appearance of the site.

The view was the best part, as far as she was concerned. Clear blue water stretched across the valley, its surface rippling in the light breeze and glinting in the sunshine. On the far side, the hills were hazy against the sky, with a hint of gold and orange showing in the green of the trees. The lake, a shimmering mirror, reflected the outline of hills and clouds. She pictured sitting on a deck with a mug of morning coffee, feeding her soul with such a glimpse of God's creation.

She looked back at the construction. Ironic, in a way, that the boy who'd never had a real home, the man who didn't bother to establish a home of his own, loved to create for others what he'd never had for himself.

Obviously the Lesters thought of their cold elegance as home. She saw again the nursery they, or their decorator, had created for Marcy, and felt a shiver of panic. Link was certainly giving Mrs. Bradshaw a lot of credit, assuming she could see through their facade to what was in Frank and Julia's hearts.

No. She couldn't let herself obsess about what was happening at the Lester house right now. She had to have faith that God would work this out.

She'd take a closer look at the houses, mud or no mud. That would occupy her mind until the moment when she had Marcy back in her arms again.

She picked her way across the torn-up earth, approaching the nearest of the buildings. It seemed to be the farthest along, with its roof nearly complete.

A movement caught her eye, and she saw Link step out onto the roof as easily as she would step onto a pavement. He walked lightly along the roof edge, emerging from shadow into sun.

The light hit him. It outlined his tall figure, glinted from his dark hair, dazzled the eye. She stopped, feeling her heart thump wildly.

Maybe being around him so much for the past week had dimmed her realization of the effect he had on her. She'd begun to take it for granted, just as the carpenters must take for granted working thirty feet from the ground.

That didn't mean it wasn't dangerous. That didn't mean falling wouldn't hurt.

The trouble was, she couldn't help it. She was falling in love with him again.

No.

The thought was so emphatic she had to look around to be sure she hadn't said it aloud. But if she had, there was no one close enough to hear.

She took a breath, trying to rein in the thoughts that galloped through her mind like runaway horses. She couldn't fall in love with Link. She couldn't. They both knew this marriage was make-believe— that it would end as soon as Marcy was safe.

She wouldn't embarrass both of them by feeling something for Link that he clearly didn't feel for her. Even if all the other good reasons why she shouldn't love him miraculously vanished, that was still plain.

What am I doing, Lord? Her prayer felt desperate. *Is this just imagination the result of being thrown so close together at such a traumatic time? Please, help me understand what's happening. Show me what to do.*

"What do you think?"

Link's question startled her so that for a moment she feared he'd seen into her thoughts. Then she realized he was talking about the building.

"It will probably be lovely when it's done." She shaded her eyes to look up at him.

He laughed, balancing on the edge of the roof in a way that made her dizzy.

"It doesn't look like anything yet, but it will." He gestured, swinging his arm wide, and her heart lurched. "There'll be a deck off the living room there, looking out over the lake."

"Wonderful." She tried to breathe. "Now, would you please come down if you're going to talk to me?"

His chuckle was warm and teasing. "Afraid of heights, Annie? I'll be down in a second." He turned to call a few instructions to one of the workmen, then swung himself onto a ladder and scrambled down.

A few feet from the ground, he paused and looked down at her, his eyes betraying amusement. "Sure you wouldn't like to come up? There's a great view from the top."

"No, thanks." She hoped her tone was prim enough to disguise the fact that she was breathless. "But don't let me keep you from anything you need to do."

He dropped to the ground next to her. "I'm finished up there, but I need to find some papers in the trailer. Come along and see what the plans look like.''

He took her arm to lead her across the rough ground to a small metal trailer set in the shade of a huge hemlock. The simple gesture sent a shiver of awareness through her.

She tried to suppress the feeling. She had to get a handle on this, right now. Being so close to Link was like juggling dynamite—sooner or later it was bound to explode.

The green-and-white construction trailer sat a little distance from the houses, looking, oddly enough, more permanent than they did. Because it was a finished work, she supposed. The houses, when they were done, would fit into the wooded landscape in a way that the metal trailer couldn't.

''Watch your step.'' Link clasped her elbow to help her up the cement block that served as a step into the trailer.

''I can manage.'' She drew free as she stepped inside. She'd better manage. She'd better find a way to erase these irrational feelings.

Being in the close confines of the trailer certainly didn't help. Drawings lined the walls, and papers covered the long table. What appeared to be some sort of legal permit was pinned above the desk.

Link seemed to fill all the available space, so that no matter where she moved, she was within a foot of him. Clearly he wasn't as bothered by this proximity as she was. He looked totally preoccupied.

"That's what the project will look like when it's finished." He nodded toward a detailed drawing that covered one wall of the trailer. "Davis did that for our presentation to the investors."

He began sorting through a stack of files on the battered desk. As she moved closer to the drawing, she realized that her imagination hadn't been good enough to do justice to the project.

Ten houses blended into the surrounding trees, looking as if they had grown there. Each was individual, yet all of them harmonized. Link and Davis had taken advantage of the uniqueness of each site, employing a wraparound deck on one house, a soaring cathedral ceiling on another.

She touched the detail of a gracefully arched deck. "It really is a wonderful plan, Link. I can see why this means so much to you."

He picked up a couple of files and joined her, his gaze fixed on the drawing. His eyes darkened, like those of a man seeing the woman he loved. He was looking at his dream.

Her throat tightened. A woman would have to be very special to compete with that.

"We wanted this project from the moment we heard the land was available. We had to sink everything we had into the property and materials, but it would be worth it. This project would put Conrad and Morgan on the map."

"Would?" Something about his tone made it sound as if the dream had receded.

He shrugged. He was so close she felt the move-ment of his shoulders.

"This was doable with Davis's help." He traced one of the houses with his fingertip, then planted his palm flat against the drawing. "We worked well to-gether. We complemented each other in a lot of ways. Without him, it's not so easy."

"But you've made a strong start. And Chet said that the board was behind the project."

"Behind the project, yes." He stared intently at the drawing, his dark eyes hooded, hiding his feelings. "Behind me? I'm not so sure."

"They must know that you're the logical person to bring this project to a conclusion. Who else would do it?"

His mouth twisted a little. "Frank would like to be the boss, even though he knows little or nothing about construction work and even less about design."

"There's your answer, then." She wanted to wipe away the tension that was evident in every line of his body. "The other investors are surely smart enough to know that about Frank."

"I hope so." He straightened, running his hand through his hair and then clasping the back of his neck. "I'd be happy just to see a little less of him. I keep finding him wandering around the site. And Vera says he's been turning up at the office when I'm not there."

"You can't keep him away?" She made it a ques-tion. At this point, anything Frank did that might have a connection with Marcy's custody was of concern to her.

He shrugged. "His seat on the board gives him access to the office and the site. What he thinks he's going to find escapes me, but it's annoying, all the same."

She rubbed her arms, thinking of Frank's smile. He made her more uneasy than annoyed.

"Are you cold?" Link put his arm around her shoulder in a quick hug.

It warmed her. Down to her toes.

"No, I'm fine." She stepped casually out of the circle of his arm, because it was too tempting just to stay there. "Just thinking about what you said."

"Look, don't start worrying." He frowned. "My part of this deal is to take care of the business, and I will. I didn't mean to upset you."

"You didn't. I want to understand." She should have made more of an effort from the beginning. "After all, this is Marcy's project, too, thanks to her father."

He nodded, his face lightening a little at the mention of the baby. "Too bad she's not as good at keeping the books as her daddy was. That's a talent that was left out of my makeup all together."

"Don't you have a bookkeeper?" She should have interested herself enough in the business to know that, at least.

"Vera does some of it, but Davis actually kept most of the records on his computer. I've been struggling to keep up with it, but half the time I can't even find the right files.'' One corner of his mouth quirked. "Give me a blueprint and I know what to do. A computer's something else again. As for a spreadsheet— forget it.''

The need might as well have been written in large letters over his head. Link needed—the company needed—something that she could very easily do. The bookkeeping he was talking about would be child's play to her. It might actually be fun.

If she offered to help, that would be one more thing bringing her close to Link. One more reason to be in his company, to be telling herself he didn't mean anything to her anymore, to know she was kidding herself.

The more she was around Link, the harder it would be to protect her heart.

Still, she couldn't escape the fact that she'd asked God to guide her in this situation. She'd always believed that if the Lord dropped a responsibility right in your lap, it was pretty safe to assume that burden was for you, whether you wanted it or not. She couldn't ignore this one.

"Why don't you let me take over the record-keeping Davis was doing?''

She couldn't mistake the relief that washed over his face. Then, almost immediately, he shook his head.

"No, that's not fair. You have all the responsibility of Marcy. I can't ask you to do this, too.''

"You didn't ask, I offered." She hoped she sounded confident. "I'd be glad to keep my hand in with something I know how to do. I can work on it in the evening after Marcy goes to bed."

"Are you sure?" He turned so that he was looking full in her face, the movement bringing him very close.

I'm sure I should be looking for ways to stay away from you, not get closer. "Yes. I mean it."

He let out his breath in a whoosh of relief. "I can't tell you how great that would be, Annie. I can work with you in the evenings on it. Maybe you can even show me how to open the spreadsheets."

"I think I can manage that." The question was, could she manage to do this and not get even more involved emotionally with Link?

That was a good question. Unfortunately, she thought she already knew the answer.

Link felt like a husband and father coming home to the family he loved. Alarms went off in his mind, and he braked so abruptly that the truck shimmied as it came to a stop in the driveway.

Unfortunately, being together every evening in the week since Annie had offered to help him with the company books had put too many thoughts in his mind that didn't belong there.

His fingers tightened on the steering wheel, and he made no effort to get out of the truck. He'd better get this straight in his mind. This wasn't real. The warm, cozy, welcoming home wasn't his—not for keeps.

Ironic, that he of all people should be put in the position of having what amounted to a counterfeit family. Maybe God was trying to tell him something.

Whatever the lesson might be, he could only assume he wasn't learning it very well. But one thing he'd better get right, and quickly. He couldn't let Annie and Marcy grow to depend on him, any more than he could depend on them. This situation was dangerous enough without that.

He slid out of the truck and walked quickly to the house, knowing how much he wanted to see them even while he was telling himself to be careful.

They were both in the family room, looking just like the cozy picture he'd been imagining. Marcy ran to him, carrying a block in each hand, and threw herself into his arms. The feel of her soft cheek against his nearly undid all his careful resolutions.

He put her down, and she held out the blocks. ''Bock,'' she announced, then ran to put them in her bright red plastic wagon. ''Bock.'' She ran to the far corner of the family room, where it looked as if a wagonload of blocks had been dumped, to pick up two more.

''She's been doing that for the last hour,'' Annie said. She was curled up in the corner of the couch, wearing jeans and that soft yellow sweater that made you want to touch it. Touch her.

Concentrate, he told himself. ''Doing what?'' He

sat down next to her, drawn by the smile that curved her mouth as she watched Marcy.

"She carries the blocks over two at a time and puts them in the wagon. Then when all the blocks are in, she pulls the wagon to the corner, dumps it and starts all over again."

"Maybe she's getting ready for her partnership in Conrad and Morgan," he said.

Annie transferred her smile to him. "It's more likely the fact that toddlers are into sorting things and putting them into containers."

"You've been reading that toddler book again, haven't you?" He reached for the volume she held in her lap. "Is that what this is?" But he realized immediately that it wasn't.

"There's no harm in reading up on the subject." She sounded a little defensive. "But no, this is one of our old family albums. I knew Becca had it somewhere. I told you we're all bringing pictures of mommy and daddy to play group tomorrow."

"I remember." He smiled, opening the album. "I also remember I promised to vacuum tonight."

"I'll hold you to it."

He leafed through the book. "Let's see which one I think you should use."

"Those are just pictures of me." She reached out to flip the page for him. "Becca is farther on."

He pulled the book out of her reach. "No harm in checking out Aunt Annie's baby pictures, is there?"

She made a soft sound that might have been disagreement but she didn't try to take the album away.

He leafed through the first few pages. "You were a cute kid." Annie had been a solemn-looking baby with dark hair that stood up in a little tuft on top of her head. After he'd turned a page or two, he realized something was missing. "I don't see your mother in any of these pictures."

Annie clasped her hands together in her lap, as if she didn't know what else to do with them. "She… My mother had to go into the hospital after I was born. She was never very strong."

He wanted to ask for details, but Annie so clearly didn't want to talk about it that he wasn't sure what to say. He turned a few more pages.

There was her mother, appearing in the photos when Annie was about six months old or so. A photo of the three of them showed Annie looking solemn, her mother strained and her father tense.

He glanced at Annie, wondering. Her face was averted, and a wing of shiny dark hair swung down over her cheek, shielding her expression.

Becca appeared on the next page—bright as a new penny, all chubby cheeks, dimples and blond curls. He looked from the photo to Marcy.

"Okay, I guess I have to give in on this one. Marcy does look like Becca did as a baby."

Annie turned back toward him, her smile flashing. "I told you."

She leaned closer, pointing to one of the pictures.

Her hair brushed his cheek, and he could smell the aroma that identified her, a clean mixture of soap and baby powder that was irrationally attractive.

"I picked this one. What do you think?" she asked.

"Cute." He glanced past the photo of Becca standing in a playpen to the next one, then found he couldn't tear his gaze away.

Annie's mother was on her knees, arms spread wide, face relaxed and lit with love. Becca, arms reaching, toddled toward her laughing.

Annie stood in the background. It was probably only the quality of the old photograph that made it look as if she stood in the shadows while the other two were in the light.

But the quality of the photograph had nothing to do with the message that her little figure communicated. She hung back, an expression of longing on her face. She clasped her hands behind her, as if unwilling to ask for something she wouldn't get.

His stomach twisted. He recognized the longing because he'd felt it himself. Annie, with her nice, ordinary, middle-class background, still hadn't had the one thing a child needed most—that sense of being loved unconditionally.

You setting up as a psychiatrist now, Morgan?

Trouble was, he couldn't jeer himself out of this. He'd seen Annie make that exact same gesture in the past few weeks, as if inside she was still that little girl who didn't think she was the loved one.

"Link?" Annie looked at him, brown eyes questioning. "Is that photo okay?"

"Yes, sure." He handed her the album, trying to dismiss his thoughts.

A man who couldn't risk loving. A woman who didn't think she could be loved. They were caught in a marriage that could cut both of them to pieces.

Chapter Nine

If she'd accepted Link's offer to go in late to work and help her get ready for play group, maybe she wouldn't be so stressed. Annie smoothed her hands down her slacks, trying to suppress the butterflies in her stomach, and assessed the kitchen and family room.

Ridiculous, to be so worried about having everything perfect for a play group. She ran through her mental checklist, grateful that Marcy was happily watching her favorite video. The fruit salad was cut up and in the fridge, the juice and coffee ready. Jenna had said she'd bring bagels and spreads.

They'd do the photo project on the folding table, and the pictures she'd chosen were already laid out. She paused, looking at the image of Becca at Marcy's age. Blond curls, big blue eyes, a happy smile. Even perfect strangers had responded to that smile, stopping Mom in the grocery store to say how beautiful Becca was.

The picture was perfect. She just couldn't help wishing that Link hadn't seen that album the night before. She'd had the sense that those pictures had revealed more about her family than she wanted him to know.

The barriers she'd been trying to hold up between her and Link kept crumbling, one by one. There didn't seem to be anything she could do about it, so maybe she'd better just concentrate on the task at hand.

She still had to put the quiche into the oven. She walked back into the kitchen and looked critically at the quiche. Not bad for her first-ever attempt to make something that complicated. She glanced at her watch. Should she start baking it yet?

A knock at the door decided her. If Jenna was here already, she may as well put it in. She slid the pan into the oven, then hurried to the door. Hopefully Jenna would be able to tell when the quiche was done.

She grasped the knob and pulled the door open. "Jenna, I—"

But it wasn't Jenna. It was Mrs. Bradshaw, looking formal and intimidating.

"Mrs. Bradshaw." She tried to keep the shock from her voice. "I didn't expect to see you this morning."

She couldn't possibly have forgotten something as

important as a visit from the social worker. What on earth was the woman doing here unannounced?

"I thought I'd drop by to see how Marcy does with her play group. I understand you're hosting it today."

How do you know that? She couldn't come right out and ask that question.

Mrs. Bradshaw raised an eyebrow, giving the impression that she tapped her foot impatiently. "May I come in?"

No. "Yes, of course." She stepped back away from the door. The butterflies in her stomach had turned into fire-breathing dragons. "I was just getting things ready for the group."

The woman greeted Marcy, then put her bag down on the sofa and glanced at Annie. "You did realize there would be unannounced visits, didn't you?"

"Actually, I didn't." Did that make her sound ill-prepared? "But you're very welcome to stay and observe or—"

Maybe she was ill-prepared. What etiquette was involved here? Did she ask the woman to stay for brunch? How were the other mothers going to react to having a social worker sit in on their play group?

"I won't stay long." Mrs. Bradshaw settled herself on the sofa as if to belie that remark. "How does Marcy feel about the play group?"

"She loves it." She brushed a strand of hair out of Marcy's face. "Don't you, sweetie?"

Please, don't let this be one of the days when

Marcy decided to get possessive about her toys. *Please, Lord, let this go well.*

The doorbell rang, and with another silent prayer she went to answer it. Jenna was first, carrying a bag from the bagel shop, but before she could unpack it, the others arrived. The room filled rapidly with the mothers' chatter and the children's squeals.

"Nothing quiet about this bunch." Jenna settled on the couch next to Mrs. Bradshaw as if she'd known her for years. "Hope you're not allergic to noise, Enid."

Her use of the first name sent an unpleasant chill down Annie's spine. Apparently Jenna knew the social worker. It was a small town, as Link kept reminding her.

"Annie?" Jenna looked concerned. "Do I smell something burning?"

"The quiche!" Annie ran to the kitchen, snatching the pot holders from the counter and yanking open the oven door. Too late.

She stared down at the blackened remains of her beautiful quiche, tears prickling her eyes. Could this morning get any worse?

A deafening clamor erupted from the ceiling smoke alarm. Most of the toddlers began to cry.

She wanted to join them. Apparently the answer was yes, it could get worse.

"Come on, Annie. It couldn't have been as bad as all that."

Link had come home from the work site early to

see how the play group had gone, since Annie had been so tense about it. He'd found Marcy peacefully napping and Annie sitting in the living room. That had been the first sign that something was wrong. They seldom used the formal room.

The second distress signal was Annie's tear-stained face. She'd tried to smile when he came in, but it had been a dismal failure.

He sat gingerly next to her on the peach-colored couch, half afraid he'd leave a mark. "It wasn't, was it? I'll bet people found enough to eat, even without the quiche."

"That's not the point." Her brown eyes were still bright with tears. "I messed up, not just in front of the play group mothers, but in front of Mrs. Bradshaw, too."

He'd rather have her annoyed with him than crying. "I don't get it. We weren't expecting her."

"She just showed up. Apparently we should have been expecting unannounced visits. She said she'd heard I was hosting the play group here, and she wanted to see how Marcy made out."

His sense of unease deepened. "How did she know about the play group being here?"

"I've no idea. She couldn't have come at a worse time. I'd just put the quiche in the oven, and having her here rattled me so much that I totally forgot about it."

They were back to the quiche again. He didn't understand why she couldn't just laugh it off, but obviously she couldn't.

"I'll bet everyone who was here had burned something at one time or another."

"That's what they said—" she wiped her eyes with the back of her hands, like a child trying to disguise her tears "—after we turned off the smoke alarm, aired the place out and got all the children to stop crying. All the women tried to make me feel better with stories of their own culinary disasters."

"There, you see." He took her hand, hoping to comfort her and not sure how. "They understood."

"They were being nice," she corrected. "They're all kind, and they were Becca's friends."

He thought about that revealing family picture he'd looked at the previous night. The relationship between Annie and Becca was more complicated than he'd realized, and he'd better be careful if he didn't want to make things worse.

Annie straightened, brushing her hair back from her face and attempting a smile. "Sorry. I didn't mean to turn the waterworks on for you. It was just such a fiasco."

He could still read the distress in her eyes, and it troubled him. "You don't have to be perfect, you know. Even Mrs. Bradshaw can't expect that."

"I hope you're right. I just wish I knew what she expected. What does she think is important? I feel as if I'm stumbling around in the dark, trying to do what Becca would do and not succeeding very well."

She looked down, clasping her hands in her lap. It reminded him of the younger Annie in the picture, hands clasped behind her, left out of the relationship between her mother and sister.

"You're not Becca," he said cautiously. "You can't—"

"Don't you think I know that?" She flared out so suddenly that her emotion shocked him. "Becca made people's eyes light up when she came in the room. I can never replace that."

"I didn't mean it that way." He felt his way through unexplored territory. "Okay, Becca was a special person. No one expects you to be just like her."

He saw the movement of the muscles in her neck, as if she had trouble swallowing. She shook her head, turning away from him again, her brief anger apparently spent. Or maybe it was that she couldn't talk about this. He put his hand tentatively on her back, feeling her tension through his palm.

"It's a good thing nobody expects that, because they'd be doomed to disappointment." She attempted another smile. "Sorry. This was a lot of fuss about a burned quiche."

"Some people probably take quiche very seriously. I'm not one of them."

He was rewarded with a smile that looked a little more genuine.

"Thanks, Link. I just wanted it to be perfect today. I guess I thought putting on the perfect play group was a way of showing how much I care about Marcy.''

He needed to find the thing that would comfort her. Then the words surfaced in his mind as if they'd been waiting for him to recognize them.

''You remember that sermon we heard last week? The one about David?''

Annie nodded, obviously perplexed. ''I remember. Samuel anointing David.''

''Garth said something about how God doesn't judge the way people do. God looks on the heart.'' He touched her cheek lightly, wanting to find a way to erase her doubts about herself. ''Anyone who looks at your heart sees how much you love that little girl, Annie. Don't ever doubt that.''

Her cheek moved against his fingers as she smiled. He felt the tension drain out of her.

''Then I guess we'd better pray that Enid Bradshaw looks with God's eyes. And that God doesn't care that I burned the quiche.''

The attempt at humor relieved him, and he realized he'd been holding his breath. One part of his mind stood back and looked at him, amazed. When had he ever worked so hard just to ease someone else's hurt?

This wasn't just someone else. This was Annie.

Thinking her name seemed to set up a vibration inside him. His palm flattened against her cheek, cradling it skin to skin. Her softness and warmth flowed into him.

''Annie.'' It was almost a whisper.

He hadn't realized how attracted to her he was. Now he did, and it scared him.

Her lashes swept up, and she looked at him, her eyes darkening. He brushed his thumb against her lips and felt them tremble.

And then he kissed her. He couldn't think, couldn't analyze pros and cons, couldn't do anything except slide his arms around her and draw her close. Her kiss was as sweet and willing as it had been all that time ago, wiping out the years between.

She touched his face, and he thought she murmured his name. He felt the hard, cool metal of the ring on her finger. His ring.

It was a dash of cold water in his face. He drew back slowly. He couldn't let Annie feel as if he rejected her. But he couldn't let this happen, either.

Talking Annie into a marriage of convenience had been the worst possible thing he could have done to her. It had just confirmed her feeling that she couldn't inspire love in the way she thought Becca had.

Her parents had harmed her. True, her mother had been sick. They'd probably done the best they could under the circumstances. But still, they'd hurt Annie.

What was it she'd said? *Becca made people's faces light up when she came into the room.*

She'd revealed so much with that simple statement. She wanted someone's face to light up for her.

And unless he knew he could be that someone, he'd better keep his hands off her.

* * *

She was swimming upward from a dream of being in Link's arms. For a moment Annie lay still in the comfortable bed, seeming to feel Link's lips on hers. Then she sat up, remembering.

Link had kissed her. Then he had put her away from him carefully and withdrawn, giving her no clue to what he was thinking.

Her throat tightened, and she frowned down at the blue-and-white patchwork quilt. What had happened? Link had had second thoughts, obviously. But why had he kissed her at all, when he so obviously felt there could be nothing between them?

Had she invited that kiss? Her cheeks went suddenly hot, and she pressed her palms against them. Maybe he'd read something in her eyes, in that moment when he was trying to make her feel better about her failure. Maybe he'd seen a longing that she was barely aware of herself.

No, that wasn't fair. She'd better be honest, at least with herself. She was aware of it, all right. In those moments at the building site she'd recognized only too well what was happening.

It *couldn't* happen. She'd let down her guard with Link once before, and he'd nearly broken her heart. Now they were trapped together in a situation that invited intimacy, and Link's withdrawal had shown her very clearly what his boundaries were.

Soft chatter from Marcy's room told her the baby

was awake. If she didn't go to her, the chatter would turn to crying.

She slipped out of bed, hurriedly pulling on jeans and a sweatshirt. Mornings were cooler now, the leaves on the maples in the square turning inexorably, even though they hadn't had a killing frost yet.

A killing frost. She paused for a moment, hand pressed against her chest, feeling as if the frost had struck there.

Selfish, some part of her scolded. *You've always known Link wasn't for you. Stop thinking about him and get on with what has to be done.*

Good advice, she thought as she went quickly across the hall to the nursery. Unfortunately, if she were able to take it, she wouldn't need it.

Hand on the nursery door, she adjusted her face. She remembered Becca saying, very seriously, that she always went in with a smile when Marcy woke up. She thought that helped account for Marcy's sunny disposition.

It couldn't hurt. She opened the door, her smile quickly turning genuine when she saw Marcy's face. Maybe it was really the other way around. Marcy's smile could touch the hardest heart.

"Good morning, sweetheart. How are you?"

Marcy dropped the teddy bear she was playing with and scrambled to her feet, holding both hands out above the crib railing. "Nan," she demanded.

Annie scooped her up, planting a kiss on the chubby cheek and feeling a flood of love. This was all she needed. She just had to concentrate on being the best mother she possibly could to Marcy. The love they'd share would be everything she could want.

She changed Marcy quickly, singing to her and laughing at her babble, then picking her up again. "Okay, let's go get some breakfast for Marcy."

When she reached the top of the stairs, she stopped. Link was still downstairs. She could hear him moving around the kitchen. She'd hoped he'd be gone by the time they went down.

Well, she wouldn't be a coward about facing him again. Arms around the baby, she went quickly down to the kitchen.

"Good morning." Link's gaze seemed to glance off hers. He took Marcy, lifting her high before giving her a hug. "How's my girl today?" He kissed her.

If Link could ignore what had happened between them, so could she. "I'll get her milk ready. She doesn't need to go in the high chair yet."

She poured milk into the blue cup that was Marcy's favorite, screwed the lid tight and put the cup into the baby's reaching hand.

Marcy stuffed the spout into her mouth and leaned against Link's shoulder, expression blissful. Link watched her, smiling.

"Wish I enjoyed my morning coffee as much as she enjoys that."

Annie poured a cup for herself from the pot he'd already made. "Do you want more?"

"No, I have to leave." He put Marcy down and

watched as she toddled into the family room. "But there's something we need to talk about first."

Apprehension gripped her heart. If he wanted to discuss that kiss—

"About Mrs. Bradshaw," hc said abruptly. "How did she know you were hosting the play group yesterday? You didn't tell her, did you?"

This she could talk about, though she didn't have any answers.

"I never mentioned it to her." She frowned. She'd been so preoccupied with the things that had gone wrong that she hadn't really given that her full attention. "It is odd, now that I think about it. Even if she knows people in the play group, why would they tell her?"

Link leaned back against the pale birch cabinet, planting his hands behind him on the edge of the counter. He should have looked relaxed but he didn't. His eyes were very serious when he stared at her.

"I don't like it, Annie." He moved his shoulders as if he felt something crawling up his back. "I think we need to find out how she knew."

"How do you expect to do that?"

"Ask her."

"You can't do that." Her response was immediate.

"Why not?" He reached out and lifted the receiver from the white phone that rested on the counter. "Seems to me the direct approach is best."

"I'm not so sure." She tried to marshal her thoughts even as she took Mrs. Bradshaw's number from the bulletin board and handed it to him. "I don't know what the etiquette is for dealing with a social worker who's investigating you. Do you?"

She wished she hadn't spoken. That had sounded unpleasantly close to a reminder of Link's childhood, even though she hadn't meant her words that way.

Link's expression didn't betray anything. If it took nerve for him to approach the woman, he didn't show it.

She was half hoping Mrs. Bradshaw wouldn't be in yet—when the woman obviously answered. Link didn't waste time on preliminaries. Before Annie could express any more reservations about this, he'd asked the question.

She waited, hands gripping each other, while he concluded the short conversation. She couldn't tell anything from his responses. If Mrs. Bradshaw was offended at his question—

He hung up and turned to her, frowning.

"What?" Her nails dug into her palms.

"She said it wasn't a secret. She happened to be talking to Julia, and Julia told her."

Julia. Her fists clenched.

"I suppose Julia thought it would be a wonderful idea for Mrs. Bradshaw to drop in at that particular moment."

He lifted an eyebrow. "We're not going to start talking about that quiche again, are we?"

She had to smile in spite of the cloud of worry that hung over her. "No more talk of burned quiches, I promise." The smile slipped away. "I can understand Julia's motives. She hoped I'd look bad if the social worker turned up and rattled me when I was entertaining. But how did Julia know about it to tell her?"

"I don't know. Yet." Link's face set in his determined, I've-decided-and-that's-it expression. "We've got to find out who's been carrying tales to Julia. It must be someone in the play group."

"I suppose you expect me to do that." Her heart shrank from trying to probe which of Becca's friends had chosen to be on the Lesters' side.

"It'll come more naturally from you than from me."

"You probably know them better than I do."

He frowned at her for another moment, then shrugged. "Okay, I'll try and ask some tactful questions, too."

On second thought, maybe relying on Link's tact wasn't such a good idea. "That's all right. I'll do it. Jenna has been the friendliest. She might have some idea."

"Good." He pushed himself away from the counter.

"We'll see a lot of people at the company picnic Saturday. It will become clear who's on Frank and Julia's side."

Some of her new-found confidence slipped away. "Do we have to go?" The thought of facing Frank and Julia and perhaps watching people line up beside them made her feel a little sick.

"Yes, of course we do." He looked at her as if she were an obstacle to be removed. "You know that."

She nodded slowly. She knew, but did Link have any idea how difficult this was for her? Maybe, or maybe not. Even if he did, it wouldn't change anything. Link charged toward his goal, carrying her along with him. She could only pray they all arrived where they had to be, with Marcy safe in her care.

Chapter Ten

It was probably better that Annie not know how much Mrs. Bradshaw's unexpected visit had bothered him, Link thought as he lifted the picnic hamper from the kitchen table. It had niggled at him for the rest of the week, and the few tactful inquiries he'd made hadn't resolved anything.

Someone close to him or to Annie had told Julia Lester about the play group meeting. Silly, on the surface, to worry about something so slight, but he didn't like it. That small betrayal might mean that the town's opinion had begun to solidify against them.

Annie didn't know how small towns worked, but he did. Lakeview could be closing ranks behind the Lesters, marking him and Annie off as outsiders.

He glanced at Annie, who was trying to persuade a wiggling Marcy into her red jacket for the company picnic. She'd been upset enough at her imagined failure with the play group. He couldn't lay another fear on her, not now. She had to be—they both had to be—convincing as a family today.

Carrying the picnic basket, he opened the family room door and bumped into a large carton on the porch. He checked the label, then glanced back into the family room.

"Were you expecting a package from your father?"

Annie's face lit up and she dropped the jacket. "Did it come already? That's great."

"I'll bring it in." He set the picnic basket on the porch and lifted the carton.

Marcy made a determined sprint toward the half-open door. Annie scooped her up, then closed the door behind him. She bounced the baby in her arms as she followed him to the kitchen table.

He set the box down. "I gather you know what this is."

"Our dollhouse." Annie was as excited as he'd ever seen her. "Dad found it in the attic and said he'd send it for Marcy. Will you take her while I open it?"

He glanced at his watch. "Can't this wait until after the picnic?" The need to get moving rode him. One way or another, he'd be able to gauge people's reactions to them today.

"We can take another few minutes, surely." She tugged at the box lid.

He opened his mouth to say no, then changed his mind. He'd rather indulge her curiosity for a few

minutes than risk making her nervous over how she'd
be received today. He pulled the penknife from his
pocket and slit the thick layer of tape.

"I didn't know you were into dollhouses. Wasn't
an abacus more your speed?"

"Actually, I had an abacus, too. Surprised?"

"Not a bit. Every budding accountant should have
one."

Annie set Marcy down, hugging herself impatiently. "The dollhouse was special. Becca and I
played with it for hours at a time. We had a whole
series of imaginary adventures with our little figures."

For once, she was talking about her sister without
sorrow darkening her eyes.

"Then, Marcy should definitely have it." He
yanked the lid free, then dumped out an armload of
packaging material, exposing a gray roof. "Here we
go." He lifted the building out, shredded paper snow-
ing onto the kitchen tile.

Annie practically danced around the table, eagerly
pulling packaging foam off the house. The tall, white,
Victorian replica had a round turret and a wraparound
porch festooned with gingerbread trim so small he
couldn't imagine someone carving it.

He whistled softly, admiring the workmanship.
"That's quite a dollhouse. It looks like something
you'd see in a museum."

"Our grandfather made it for us." Annie touched
a broken porch railing, and some of the light faded

from her eyes. "I didn't realize it was in such bad shape. I knew the furniture was broken, but I hoped the house itself would just need cleaning up. I can't let Marcy play with this."

"I'll fix it." He heard the words come out of his mouth and couldn't remember forming the thought. What did he mean, he'd fix it?

"Do you think you can?" Hope softened her face, then faded quickly. "You don't have time, do you?"

No.

"I'll make time." It was a small enough thing to do for her. "You've been making time to work on the books, haven't you? So I'll work on the dollhouse." He swung a tiny shutter. "It's not as bad as it looks. Your grandfather was a good craftsman."

"I don't remember him very well. He died when I was about five or six." She touched the turret lovingly. "But I remember the fun we had with this."

"Reason enough." He picked Marcy up, showing her the dollhouse. "We'll make it as good as new."

Marcy didn't seem impressed by the promise. She reached toward the house, then pulled her hand back.

But Annie—Annie's face was lit with happiness. A man would be a fool not to try and keep that look on her face.

Link pulled into the lot at the lakeside park, noticing the number of cars already there. They were late. If people wanted to talk about them, they'd had plenty of opportunity. He opened the door.

Annie slid out quickly enough, but he could sense hesitation as they started unloading. He studied her averted face, his gaze touching the line of her cheek and the set of her chin. Even without understanding small-town dynamics, she didn't like walking into a crowd of people she didn't know. Whether some of her nervousness resulted from their need to look like a happily married couple, he wasn't sure.

He tossed a blanket over his shoulder to free up his hand, and then clasped hers.

"It's okay," he said, trying to sound reassuring in spite of his own doubts. "They're nice folks."

She glanced sideways at him. "I'd like to take your word for it, but will Frank and Julia be here?"

He understood that concern, at least. "Frank's only concern is with impressing the board, not the ordinary working people. They won't be here."

The lines in her forehead smoothed. "Let's go pretend we're a happy family, then."

They walked across the grass toward the group gathered at the pavilion. He put Marcy down, and she scuffed through the carpet of fallen leaves.

The aroma from the charcoal grills floated teasingly toward them, but it didn't look as if anyone had started cooking yet. Some of the guys were playing volleyball at a net they'd set up. Link started toward it. When Annie hesitated, he glanced at her.

"Don't you want to play?"

"I'm not much for volleyball." She took the blanket from his shoulder and nodded toward a woman with a child along the sideline. "Marcy and I will join the audience."

He almost let her walk off alone.

"Hey." He scooped Marcy up and put her on his shoulder. "I might not be the most sensitive guy in the world, but at least I'll take you over there."

"Sounds pretty sensitive to me."

They walked around the improvised court, and he responded in kind to some good-natured ribbing about the newlyweds arriving late and whether or not he was in shape for the game.

He tossed the blanket down next to Linda Trent, relieved that it was she. At least Annie had met her.

"You remember Linda, don't you? We ran into her and Joe at the Town House the other night."

"Sure. She's in the play group, too." Annie dropped down onto the blanket, pulling Marcy close as Linda's toddler dived at her. "It's nice to see someone I know."

He stood still, frowning. Linda was avoiding his eyes. That wasn't a good sign.

"You can go play volleyball, Link—"

That might have been a warning in Annie's words. Maybe she understood more than he'd thought. "Linda and I will chat."

Quickly, before he could think too much about it, he bent and dropped a quick kiss on her lips.

"Have fun, sweetheart. It won't take me long to beat these guys."

Her color rose. "See that you do. We'll be cheering for you."

He jogged onto the court, trying to beat down his concern. No good would come of his confronting Linda. Little as he liked relying on anyone else, he'd have to trust Annie's judgment on this one.

Somewhat to his surprise, he did.

Annie watched him jog onto the court. The other men greeted him easily, apparently not feeling any barriers between them even though Link was their boss.

Did Link realize how they accepted him, or was that acceptance so routine that he didn't even think about it anymore? The little he'd told her about his childhood had shown her how much he valued belonging here.

He'd certainly picked up quickly enough on Linda's uneasiness. She'd seen it in his eyes.

Little Charlie made another determined dive at Marcy, and Linda pulled him back onto her lap. "Marcy doesn't want a hug, sweetie."

Annie shook a bag of blocks out onto the blanket. "Why don't you two play blocks? Marcy, help Charlie build a tower."

The blocks distracted the children, for the moment at least, and Annie smiled at Linda. "It's so nice to see you. I was afraid I wouldn't know a soul here."

Should she ask Linda right out about Julia? If

Linda had already chosen sides, that might be the worst thing she could do.

Give me the words, Lord. I don't know how to approach this.

"Everyone knows who you are." Linda helped her son put one block on top of another. "I'm sure they're ready to get acquainted."

"I appreciate that." How open should she be? "I thought maybe, with the custody case going on, people might find it awkward to be friendly."

"Because of the Lesters?" Something shadowed Linda's dark eyes. "I don't think so."

She sounded reassuring, but a faint hint of some other emotion disturbed Annie. What *wasn't* Linda saying?

Cheers and jeers erupted on the volleyball court, and Linda's husband, Joe, pounded Link on the back. Apparently he'd done something good. Link's face, split by a grin, looked younger—like that of the boy she'd known once. Fallen in love with, once.

She shoved that thought out of her mind. She had enough worrying her without dwelling on that.

"I've been hoping that Becca and Davis's friends, like you and Joe, would feel that Link and I are the right people to have Marcy," she said carefully.

"Of course we do." Linda said it so quickly that nervousness seemed to drive the words.

Annie's apprehension deepened. All her natural reticence urged her to let the subject drop, but a stronger instinct pushed her forward. Maybe that feeling was the guidance she'd prayed for.

She put her hand over Linda's where it lay on the blanket. "What is it, Linda? Something's obviously bothering you."

Linda bit her lip, looking at her with such a guilty expression that Annie sensed what was coming before the woman spoke.

"I...I didn't mean to. But I think I did something wrong."

"This is about Mrs. Bradshaw showing up at play group, isn't it."

Linda nodded, blinking back tears. "I'm sorry. Really I am. I didn't know that was why she was being so nice to me. I should have realized she was up to something."

Julia, obviously. Tension was an icy ball in her stomach. "What happened?"

"I ran into her—Julia, I mean—at the grocery. She's never done more than nod at me, but that day she stopped, said how cute Charlie was." Linda flushed. "I guess I was flattered that she wanted to talk to me. She asked about the play group."

"And you told her when it met and that it would be at my house."

Linda nodded miserably. "I'm so sorry. I didn't realize she meant mischief. But then, when the social worker showed up, I figured Julia must have told her." She grasped Annie's hand. "I really am sorry. I wanted to tell you but I just couldn't."

And Annie wanted to be angry, but she couldn't. "It wasn't your fault. You couldn't have known." She tried to smile. "Anyway, I was the one who messed up, not you. You could probably have juggled the play group, the brunch *and* Mrs. Bradshaw without batting an eyelash."

Linda didn't respond with a smile. Instead, her eyes filled with tears. "I'd never want to do anything to hurt you. Honest. After the second chance Link gave my Joe, we'd do anything for him."

"Second chance?"

"Link didn't tell you?"

Annie shook her head. She didn't want to admit how many things she and Link hadn't shared.

"Joe is an alcoholic," Linda said simply. "He hasn't had a drink in years, and I know he won't again. But one time he messed up, showed up at work drunk and nearly caused an accident. Most people would have fired him without a thought. Not Link. He sobered him up, got him to rehab, even kept paying his salary until he could work again. We can never thank Link enough for that."

"I didn't know." It was another insight into her husband, and one she hadn't expected.

"Anyway, we're on your side." Linda clasped her hand. "I'll do anything to make up for telling Julia. Anything."

Annie had to blink back tears. "It's all right. Really." Oddly enough, she felt as if she'd made a friend.

* * *

"Okay, smile!" Annie sighted through the view-finder and clicked the camera button, hoping she actually got a picture. The old-fashioned wooden carousel swung Link and Marcy past her as she lowered the camera, but she caught a glimpse of the baby's laughing face.

She'd try again the next time they came around. The music tinkled happily, the painted wooden horses moved up and down. Link had told her it was one of the oldest wooden carousels in the country still in operation. Watching it was like watching a piece of the past.

Link and Marcy came into view again as the carousel slowed. She snapped two more pictures in quick succession. Marcy didn't show a bit of fear at being atop the glossy palomino. She laughed, waving both arms wildly, obviously perfectly secure with Link's hands holding her.

They looked right together. She grappled with that thought as the carousel stopped and Link carried Marcy toward her. It seemed somehow disloyal to Davis and Becca, to be thinking how right they were together. Besides—

"What are you looking so solemn about?" Link lowered Marcy into her stroller. "She loved it."

"I was just hoping I actually got a picture of how much she loved it. I'm not exactly the world's greatest photographer." She fell into step as Link started pushing the stroller along the path. "But actually, there's something I need to tell you. Can we wait a bit to rejoin the others?''

He nodded. ''Let's take a walk.''

She had to tell him what she'd learned. She could only hope he wouldn't overreact.

''It was Linda. She's the one who told Julia about the play group.''

''How do you know?'' His hands tightened on the stroller handle and his jaw tensed.

''She told me.'' Annie hurried her words. ''She really didn't mean to do anything wrong. Julia wormed the facts out of her without Linda realizing what was going on.''

''That sounds like Linda. She always thinks the best of people.''

''You're not angry, are you?''

He shook his head, but she sensed something held back.

''Not at Linda. Now Julia—I suspect Julia knew just what she was doing when she suggested the social worker stop over at that particular time. She probably knew it might upset you to have Mrs. Bradshaw showing up the first time you hosted the play group.''

''It's kind of a creepy feeling.'' The breeze sent a shower of golden leaves skittering across the path, and she had to push her hair back out of her face. ''Knowing there's someone who's—well, wishing you ill.''

He looked as if he were considering her words. ''I

don't think it's as active a feeling as that where you're concerned. They just want you out of their way.''

''But Frank really does dislike you.'' She hadn't thought it through, but she realized it was true as soon as she said the words.

''I'd say so.'' Link stopped the stroller where the grassy area sloped into the trees. A trail led on into the woods along a stream, disappearing around a steep curve in the hill.

''Why?''

He shrugged. ''He has ever since Davis and I went into business together. Actually, I think he resented Davis from the day he was born. Our success, whatever it amounts to, made him worse.'' He reached out to take her hand. ''I'm afraid you just got added onto his dislike for me.''

She ought to pull her hand free. She didn't want to.

He nodded toward the trail. ''Are you up for a walk? I promise you, there's something special at the end of the trail.''

''It looks too rough for the stroller.''

''I'll put Marcy in the carrier on my back.'' He pulled the carrier from the stroller basket as he spoke.

''In that case, sure.'' She shouldn't be taking advantage of another excuse to be alone with Link, but they were together so much anyway that it hardly seemed worth the effort to try and impose limits.

She helped him adjust the carrier, and then lifted

Marcy to his back. The baby pounded her small hands on his shoulders, bouncing eagerly.

"I think she's looking forward to a hike," Annie said. "What about the stroller? We can't just leave it here."

"Sure we can." He shook his head in mock sadness. "You keep forgetting you're not in the city now. No one will bother it."

"You're right. Things are different in Lakeview."

No one would steal a stroller from the park. That was a positive, certainly. The clannishness she'd seen in the people here might be a negative, at least where she was concerned, but she thought of Linda's caring and felt a little better.

Link walked easily up the trail, even with Marcy on his back, and she followed.

"Linda told me about what you did for her husband."

He shrugged. "Joe's a good worker. I didn't want to lose him. He's proved himself since then."

She didn't think that was all of it. "Some employers wouldn't have given him a chance to prove himself."

He was quiet for a moment, and she thought he wasn't going to answer. Then he glanced back over his shoulder. "A few people gave me a chance to prove myself. I figured I ought to pass it on." He lengthened his stride, and she sensed that was all he intended to say.

The path grew narrower and steeper, and conversation would have been difficult if he'd wanted to talk. Steep cliffs of gray shale rose on both sides, and the path twisted to follow the rushing stream.

Link looked over his shoulder again. "This is Eagle Glen. Are you okay to go on?"

"Fine. It's very pretty." Actually, it was a little scary. The valley was so narrow that the sound of the water seemed to fill it.

Pale green moss covered the lower part of the cliffs, with tiny lavender and white wildflowers growing improbably in the smallest of niches. A fragment of verse passed through her mind. *"He hideth my soul in the cleft of the rock."*

Link paused. "Need a breather?"

"I'm okay." Except that she did sound breathless.

He grinned. "It's just a little farther."

"Lead on."

A few more yards and the path rounded a sheer buttress of gray rock. Beyond it—

Annie stopped, amazed. No wonder the water had sounded so loud. The stream widened out to a shallow pool, rimmed by flat gray rocks. Above the pool, a waterfall cascaded from the top of surrounding cliffs.

She tilted her head back. "It's astonishing."

Link smiled, obviously pleased with her reaction. "Eagle Falls. It's one of the highest falls on the east coast. Higher than Niagara, although it doesn't have that volume of water."

High, high above them she could see a sliver of sky. A tree, bright with autumn gold, leaned over the top of the cliffs. Its leaves drifted down like golden rain onto the still pewter pool beneath.

Annie's throat grew tight. The towering gray walls might have been a Gothic cathedral. "It's like—"

"A church," he finished for her. "That's what I always think when I come here. God's own creation."

"Yes." The word came out in a whisper.

Lord, I think we both feel Your presence here. She realized she didn't know what specifically to pray for, but that didn't seem to matter. *Please, guide our steps.*

For a long moment she just looked at Link, feeling as if they existed, for once, in perfect harmony.

Chapter Eleven

"**G**ood night, little sweetheart."

Link lowered Marcy into the crib. She snuggled down, curling one arm around her teddy bear, her body relaxing and her eyes drifting shut.

He patted her, humming softly, knowing she didn't need it but wanting to prolong the sweet moments. He looked back with faint surprise at the man he'd been just a few short weeks ago—the man who hadn't even been able to put a baby to bed.

Confidence made the difference—both his own confidence that he could do this and Marcy's confidence in him. It surprised him how much pleasure he took from this simple accomplishment.

He switched off the elephant lamp, leaving a small pink night-light burning, and slipped quietly from the room.

The old house was Sunday-evening quiet, with Annie out to Bible study and Marcy asleep. The house seemed to settle around him, as if it had become used to his alien presence, accepting him even though he wasn't a Conrad.

He went slowly down the stairs to the family room. *Family.* The word lingered in his mind.

What was God trying to teach him?

He'd put Annie's dollhouse on the folding table so he could work on it at odd moments. He picked up the tiny stair rail he'd glued together—then felt as if he were standing back and looking at himself.

Putting a baby to bed. Mending a dollhouse. Sure looked like a family man to him. He stifled the little voice that said appearances were deceiving, and pulled the lamp closer so he could get a better angle on the dollhouse's interior. He began fitting the railing back into place.

The door swung open. Annie came in with a gust of rain. She shook out her umbrella and propped it in the corner.

"You're working on the dollhouse." Her face lit with so much pleasure that it warmed him.

"I had a little time to spare after I got Marcy down." He leaned back in the chair, watching as Annie shed her jacket and fluffed rain-dampened hair.

She came toward him. "Did she go down all right?"

"Without a murmur."

Her smile seemed to congratulate him. She rested her hand on the back of his chair as she leaned over to peer into the dollhouse. He caught a whiff of her light, fresh scent and felt the moist brush of her hair against his cheek.

"You've done so much already. I never dreamed you could repair all the damage. I'd have given up." She glanced at him, her face very close.

He managed to take a breath without strangling. If she had any idea how much he wanted to kiss her, she'd fly across the room.

"Wait until I give it a fresh coat of paint. It'll look like new."

She ran the tip of her finger along the wooden mantelpiece. "There used to be a picture in a miniature frame over the mantel. I'll see if I can find something, but it will have to be attached so Marcy can't pull it loose."

"I can do that." He studied her face. She looked lost in memories. "What about furniture? And dolls?"

"I'll look for things that are big enough to be safe for an almost-two-year-old. I remember—"

"What?" *What's put that look of sadness in your eyes, Annie?*

"We had a family of dolls that fit the house—father, mother, two sisters, and a baby that Becca insisted was a brother named Tommy."

"No chance of a real baby brother, I take it?" He put the question cautiously, still not sure what she found unhappy in these reminiscences.

"My mother was hospitalized for severe depression

several times, and I imagine my parents decided it was too difficult to have any more children. As it was, my father had his hands full taking care of us.''

He'd once assumed that Annie and Becca had had the perfect childhood. He'd been wrong.

''Weren't there any relatives who could help?''

Annie shook her head. ''Not any who lived close. And Daddy never wanted to send us away. We managed. I looked after Becca.''

When did you have a chance to be a little girl, Annie?

She touched one of the upstairs rooms. ''This was the girls' room. Every night, Becca would bring the mommy doll in here to kiss them good-night. I guess it was her way of coping when our mother was away.''

Unable to resist, he captured her hand in his. ''How did you cope, Annie?''

She looked surprised. ''I had Becca to take care of.''

''You were a child yourself.'' He thought about Marcy, sleeping securely in her crib in spite of all that had happened in her young life. ''You needed someone to kiss you good-night, too.''

He realized the words were a mistake as soon as he spoke. They made him too aware of her closeness in the quiet room. Her lips parted, and he remembered how they tasted. The slightest movement by either of them and they'd be in each other's arms again.

Annie drew back, a flush warming her cheeks.

"You—you must find it odd to be working on an old-fashioned Victorian."

She spoke as if any subject would do to fill up the silence they might otherwise fill with a kiss.

"All of your houses are modern, aren't they?"

If that was how Annie wanted it, he couldn't do anything but go along. "It's not really so different, except in style. The Victorians built homes for the way people lived then. I build homes for the way people live now. I've liked the Victorian style since I was a kid."

He stopped. Only the silence and the need to ease Annie's obvious discomfort would send him down that road of memory.

"Why is that?"

She was clearly confident that he'd share his thoughts with her. Maybe she had the right to expect that. They'd come a long way in a few short weeks.

He propped his elbows on the table, frowning at the dollhouse's gingerbread trim. He reached out to touch it lightly.

"I remember a street lined with houses like this." He shook his head. "I'm not sure where. Maybe in northwestern Pennsylvania."

She was silent, but her very stillness seemed to force him to continue.

"The street might have been Maple, or Chestnut. Streets like those were usually named for trees, I decided."

"Streets like those?"

"The kind of street where the houses had been there for a hundred years or so. The kind of street where real families had lived in real houses for generations."

He shrugged, trying to shake off the heaviness of the memory. "I must have been about eight the first time I noticed a neighborhood like that. Then I figured out that every new town we went to had one, and I started looking for them."

That search had been a relief, in a way, from the succession of dingy apartments and dingier motels he and his mother had lived in. He'd been dreaming, but they hadn't been bad dreams. When his mother was drinking, he could always go out and walk by those houses.

Annie put her hand on his shoulder. He felt her warmth permeate his shirt and touch his skin.

"I'd look at the lights and try to figure out what kind of people lived in houses like that." He'd imagined what it would be like to belong there, among the lucky ones. He shrugged, uncomfortably aware of how much he was revealing. "Kid stuff, I guess. Wanting what's on the other side of the fence."

"That's why you went into building, isn't it?" Her words arrowed right into his heart. "So you could create the thing you didn't have."

Annie heard her own words and was aghast at her temerity. How could she have asked Link something so personal? The lines in their relationship had blurred in the past weeks, but she shouldn't be pressing into an area that was not only private but probably also painful.

"I'm sorry." She clenched the hand she'd rested on his shoulder, her nails biting into her palm. "I shouldn't have said that. It's none of my business."

Link shook his head slowly. "It's okay." He looked surprised at himself. "I don't know that I ever thought of it that way, but maybe you have a point. Homes have always fascinated me—not skyscrapers or institutions. Just homes for ordinary people to live in."

Her throat had gone tight with tension, and she tried to speak naturally. "That's a very worthwhile thing. Homes should be beautiful as well as functional."

"I always felt that if I could get the—" He stopped, seeming at a loss for words, and made an amorphous shape with his hands.

"Well, the shell of the house, but not just that. If I could get the physical structure right, it ought to help ensure happiness for the people who live there." He shrugged, one corner of his mouth lifting in a half smile. "Or maybe I'm just being self-important about what I do."

"It's not self-important to put your best self into your work." Tears stung her eyes. "That's why the lakeside project is going to be so beautiful."

His mouth firmed. "I hope so. Davis and I felt good about what we were doing there. It always meant something special to me, but now—well, now, it's like I have to finish it to fulfill Davis's dream, as well as my own.''

''You've come a long way.'' Did he realize how far?

He leaned back, fixing his gaze on her face. ''You know what I wanted when I was a kid, Annie. Your turn. What did you want?'' He lifted one hand, palm out. ''And don't tell me you wanted to take care of Becca. I already know that. What did you want for Annie?''

Her mind scrambled to come up with something. She couldn't say some routine childhood wish, like a pony, not when he'd opened his heart to her. And then it popped into her mind, as if it had been there all along.

''You'll laugh,'' she warned. ''It wasn't a very worthy ambition.''

He took her hand, holding it lightly. She knew he'd let her go at the slightest indication, but she didn't move.

''Tell me.''

''I always wanted to be like Becca.'' She felt her cheeks grow warm, and she knew she was figuring this out as she went along. ''Well, you knew her. Everyone loved Becca. She just radiated warmth, and people were drawn to her. I wanted to be like that but I didn't know how. I still don't. I think it's something you're either born with or not.''

He enveloped her hand in both of his, and she felt

protected. "You're talking about your parents, aren't you?"

She had to nod. "Yes." It was hard to speak around the lump in her throat. "They love me, of course. But Becca made their faces light up. And mine, too." She smiled, remembering. "We were never competitive, like sisters sometimes are when they're close in age. You know, she even got me a date for the prom. She said if I didn't go, she wouldn't. That was Becca. She'd do anything for people she loved."

"She was one of a kind," Link said quietly. His grip tightened. "But so are you." He lifted her hand between his and kissed it. The touch of his lips moved straight from her hand to her heart. "I'd say both the Gideon girls turned out pretty special."

Her heart seemed to swell. Did he really mean that?

Maybe it didn't matter. He'd said it, and that should be enough for her.

The careful defenses she'd kept around her heart for so long crumbled into dust. She'd given away too many pieces to Link in the past few weeks. Would there be anything left of her when their time together came to an end?

That thought was still in the back of Annie's mind a few days later, much like the pot of potatoes she had simmering on the back stove burner. It didn't require looking at all the time, but it was there.

She glanced into the family room to be sure Marcy

was still safely occupied with her easel and crayons. Marcy loved to color, but was just as likely to color her way off the easel and onto the surrounding furniture if not watched. She hadn't given Becca enough credit for her ability to do so many things at once.

In a way, things had been better since that conversation with Link on Sunday night. It was as if, with his secrets out in the open, Link could relax.

She wished she could do the same. The little worm of worry came out when she least expected it. She understood why the project was so important to him—it was his measure of success. She just couldn't help but wonder how he'd take it if something went wrong.

At least the latest visit from Mrs. Bradshaw had gone well. She'd happened to arrive when Marcy was in her sunniest mood, and the house, for once, had been cleaned up enough to look passable. She'd seemed impressed by the photo album they'd started putting together, and had actually smiled warmly at Annie when she left, as if with approval.

Voices from the porch startled her, and she turned down the burner under the chicken. Marcy beat her to the door and threw herself at Link as soon as he opened it.

Link grabbed her, tossing her in the air, and Jenna came through the door behind him, laughing at the sight.

"I met Jenna at the curb," Link said. He perched Marcy on his shoulder. "She was afraid she'd interrupt our dinner, but I said we always have time for her.''

''Of course we do.'' Annie held out her hand to the woman who'd been Becca's close friend. ''Come sit down.''

''I can't stay long.'' Jenna closed the door behind her, and Annie realized she looked worried. ''But I just had to talk to you.''

Something was wrong. Annie gestured toward the couch, then sat down next to Jenna. She didn't know what, but something was wrong. Link plopped Marcy down beside her easel and came to sit on the arm of the sofa, his hand resting on Annie's shoulder as if for support. So he had the same instinct.

Jenna bit her lip, a frown line forming between her brows. ''I've been worrying about this since last night. And praying, too.'' She gave them a ghost of a smile. ''Pastor Garth would say I should have prayed first, and then I wouldn't have to worry.''

''What is it? Has something happened?'' Annie's hands knotted together.

''Maybe it's not important, but—well, you know the church supper was last night.''

Annie nodded. ''We were going to go, but Link got stuck at the project. And Marcy didn't take a very good nap. She was so tired I was afraid she'd have a meltdown if I took her out.''

''Believe me, I know how that can be.'' Jenna rolled her eyes. ''Anyone who's ever had kids would understand.''

Link's hand tightened on her shoulder. "But somebody didn't understand, I take it."

"I don't want to feel like I'm telling tales, but anyone could have heard them. Julia and Frank, I mean."

Something cold seized Annie's heart. "What did they say?"

"That you weren't even trying to be part of the community." Jenna's cheeks flushed. "I know that's not true, but I'm afraid maybe some other people don't. Then Frank said you planned to run back to Boston as soon as the hearing is over, so you don't even want to make friends here."

Annie felt as if she'd taken a blow. "Jenna, I—"

Jenna reached across to hug her. "You don't need to explain anything to me. We're friends, whatever the Lesters say." She clasped Link's hand. "Both of you."

It was a good thing Jenna didn't expect her to explain, because she couldn't. She could just hug her back and try not to cry.

Jenna released her at last. "Look at us, being silly." She got up quickly. "Listen, I have to get home to my family, but I wanted you to know. Remember, I'm on your side."

Link followed her to the door and held it for her. "Thanks, Jenna. You're a good friend."

She patted his cheek and then hurried out the door, obviously relieved that this was over.

Annie got to her feet as Link closed the door. "I'm sorry. This is my fault." She shook her head. "I should have gone, even if you couldn't. If I'd been there—''

''If you'd been there, Frank and Julia would have found another way to spread a little poison about us.'' Link's matter-of-fact tone didn't leave any room to argue. ''That's how they are. We can't stop them from talking.''

She rubbed her forehead. ''It's not just the Lesters. What about people like Jenna? She's standing up for us, when we're really planning to do just what the Lesters are accusing us of. I feel like such a fraud.''

Link caught her hands, pulling her to face him. ''Would you rather lose Marcy?'' he said bluntly. ''Because that's what we're talking about here.''

''No, of course not.'' She yanked her hands free. ''Marcy is worth anything. But that doesn't keep me from feeling like a rat for lying to Jenna.''

''You didn't lie to her. You just didn't tell her everything.''

''Isn't that the same thing?''

Link drove his hand through his hair. ''Annie, listen, I can't say this is all okay. Lord knows, I struggle with it, too. But we knew that going in. We decided this was what we had to do. That hasn't changed.''

Remorse still pricked her, but Link was right. They couldn't confide in anyone, not even Jenna. They could only keep going and hope the hearing went their way.

A chill touched her. Time was ticking away.

''It's only a little over a week until the hearing.

What if Mrs. Bradshaw hears what the Lesters are saying?''

He shrugged. ''They've probably already said it to her. We just have to hope she's wise enough to take whatever they say with a grain of salt.''

Hope. Lord, I've been hoping, but I'm afraid.

''We have to do something,'' she said. ''We have to. But what can we do to counteract rumors?''

Link gave her a grim smile. ''We're going to do something. We're going to beat the Lesters at their own game.''

She didn't think she liked the sound of that. ''How? What are you thinking?''

''Saturday night is the Downtown Business Association's annual dinner dance. Frank and Julia are the co-chairs, as a matter of fact.''

''What does that have to do with us?''

''We're going to it, that's all.''

''But how can we? Isn't that just for members?''

He gave her a look of exaggerated patience. ''The office of Conrad and Morgan is downtown, remember? Davis and I took out a membership, even though we've never been very involved. I'll stop by tomorrow and get our tickets.''

''I still don't see what that will prove.''

''It will show people we're members of the business community. It will show that we're a couple.''

Marcy flung herself at Link's legs just then, as if giving her approval of his plan. He swung her into the air.

"Link and Nan are going to a party, sweet girl. Nan's going to get dressed up and be the prettiest woman there."

It was a sign of how far he'd come into her heart that his words made her glow with pleasure in spite of her reservations about this scheme.

"I'm not so sure about that." She fell back on the oldest excuse in the world. "Besides, I didn't bring anything with me suitable to wear."

"Then, you and Marcy better take a walk downtown tomorrow and pick out something pretty."

His smile was confident, as if he knew she'd do what he wanted her to.

"Relax, Annie. It may not be the high school prom, but it will be fun. And our presence will tell anyone who's interested that Mr. and Mrs. Link Morgan are for real."

Unfortunately, they weren't. But she knew she'd go along with Link's idea anyway, because there didn't seem to be any other way.

Chapter Twelve

The ringing of the doorbell on Saturday evening made Annie's stomach turn over, and she stopped at the top of the stairs, gripping the banister. She could see the lights from the family room below, hear the sound of Link's footsteps as he went to the door.

The doorbell's ring meant that Nora was here to baby-sit with Marcy. In a few minutes she and Link would be on their way to the dinner dance he'd talked her into attending.

She pressed her hand against her stomach, hoping to calm herself. The soft coral silk of the new dress she'd bought felt smooth and comforting against her palm. Jenna had gone shopping with her, helping her to choose a dress that was perfectly suited to the occasion. Now if only she could live up to the dress.

Who was she trying to fool? This wasn't just a

question of attending a social event. This evening was far more important than that.

The custody hearing raced toward them like a tornado set on obliterating everything in its path. In less than a week, for good or ill, this would be over.

Would it be better or worse to have an idea where they stood with the social worker? She wasn't sure—didn't know if she wanted to find out, even if she could.

She seemed to be groping through a fog, trying to find the landmarks that would tell her she was on the right path. But she couldn't. She didn't even know, at this point, what was important.

This dinner dance? Link seemed to think so. She took a deep breath, trying to calm her skittish nerves.

Lord, I'm scared again. You must be tired of hearing me say that. I wish I felt that perfect confidence other Christians seem to have, but I don't.

Maybe that wasn't entirely true. She did feel confident that fighting for Marcy was the thing God wanted her to be doing.

It's not the cause that's troubling me, Father. Please, show me how to fight this battle in the way that You intend me to.

She took a deep breath and started down the stairs.

Nora was handing her jacket to Link. ''My goodness, but it's crisp outside.'' She swung toward Annie, her blue eyes sparkling. ''Annie, you look a picture. Doesn't she, Link?''

Annie felt her cheeks heat as he obediently looked, smiling a little.

"A very pretty picture," he said. He shoved the sleeve of his dark suit jacket back to check his watch. "And it's time we were on our way."

Marcy, already in her pajamas, trotted to Nora. "Car," she announced, holding up her toy car.

Nora sat down on the rug beside her "Aren't you just the smartest girl in the whole wide world." She hugged her. "Well, get along with you. Marcy and I will be fine."

Now that the moment had come, Annie was even more reluctant to leave. She knelt next to the baby. "Give Nan a hug, sweetheart."

The feel of the baby's soft arms around her neck nearly threw her off balance. She didn't want to leave her. She had to.

Link held out her coat. She stood, slipping her arms into the sleeves. He settled the coat around her and gave her shoulders a little squeeze, as if he sensed her nerves and wanted to reassure her.

"Nora knows everything there is to know about taking care of Marcy, and I've written the phone numbers down for her." His grip tightened for an instant. "Everything will be fine."

"I know." She managed to produce a smile. "Thank you again, Nora."

Nora waved off her thanks. "You two just go and have a good time."

Right, a good time. She let Link take her arm and

pilot her out the door and to the car. It wasn't so easy to have a good time when she felt as if people would be watching their every move.

Link settled behind the wheel. "You didn't want to leave her." He sounded sure.

"No."

They both knew why she didn't want to leave Marcy. They both knew that if the hearing went against them, she'd be leaving Marcy for good.

Link let the silence stretch for a few moments as he drove down Main Street and turned onto Lakeside Drive. He gave her a fleeting look, as if measuring her mood.

"Have you been out to the Lakeside Inn before?"

He was making conversation, she supposed, in an effort to distract her.

"I've seen it from the outside when Becca showed me around the area." She had a vague image of a sprawling old-fashioned lodge hovering on the shore of the lake.

"It's the only place around that's big enough for an affair like this." He leaned forward, pointing through the windshield. "There, you can see it now."

The road curved along the lake, and just ahead of them a small headland thrust out into the water. The Lakeside Inn sat at the very end, every window sparkling with white lights.

"It looks like a fairy-tale castle."

Link turned into the lane, and the trees momentarily obscured the inn from view. "Then, you must be

Cinderella,'' he said, and pulled to a stop in the parking lot.

The walkway to the inn's entrance led through a band of trees sparkling with small white lights, and the building itself was even bigger than she'd thought from a distance. Wooden additions flanked a center section of stone, capped by red chimneys and turrets.

She'd been right. It did look like a castle. And judging by the state of her nerves, she must be facing a dragon.

Link put his arm around her as they mounted the stone steps. He pulled the massive door open. ''You'll be fine,'' he murmured. ''Stop worrying.''

''If I could stop worrying on command, I'd have done it already.''

He flashed her a grin. ''Okay, that was dumb, I admit it. I just want you to relax.''

She surrendered her coat to Link, and then waited while he took it to the cloakroom. An enormous fire roaring in one of the biggest fireplaces she'd ever seen warmed the lobby in spite of high ceilings and a soaring staircase.

She heard the murmur of voices and the strains of music in the distance, coming from what must be the dinner dance. Her nerves tightened.

Link walked toward her across the lobby. He spent so much time in work clothes that his dark suit should have sat uncomfortably on him, but it didn't. He looked elegant and accomplished, like any successful businessman walking into an event where he knew he'd be welcomed and admired.

He took her arm. "The Adirondack Room is around the corner. Sounds as if most people are here already."

"Does that mean we're making an entrance?" Her steps slowed involuntarily as they rounded the corner. For a moment they were alone—the lobby out of sight behind them, the ballroom hidden around another corner.

Link stopped, looking down at her. "Still nervous?"

"A little," she admitted. "Everyone's going to be looking at us. Wondering."

His mouth curved in an easy grin, and she realized he was enjoying this. To Link, this night was a challenge, and Link loved challenges.

"They're going to be wondering how I managed to snag the prettiest woman in town."

She looked up at him, startled, a protest on her lips. She didn't have a chance to utter it.

Almost before she realized his intent, he touched her cheek, tilted her face up and kissed her.

The stone floor was suddenly unsteady, and she put her hands on his arms for balance. He seemed to take that as an invitation, his palms moving on the soft silk as he drew her even closer. His mouth was firm, seeking, and she could no more pull away than she could fly.

His lips moved to her cheek, and his breath was as

ragged as her own. "Maybe we'd better go in before I get carried away," he murmured.

She drew back as far as his arms would let her, knowing her cheeks must be fiery. "Maybe so."

Maybe we've already been carried away.

He straightened his tie and touched a handkerchief to his lips. Then he held his arm out to her with a brilliant smile. "Ready, Cinderella?"

Ready or not. She took his arm and let a wave of emotion carry her into the room.

Link realized he felt unaccountably buoyed by that kiss, as they swept through the doors to the Adirondack Room. Felt, in fact, as if he could lick all comers.

That certainly hadn't been in his mind at the moment he'd known he was going to kiss Annie. As they'd approached the room he'd felt the tiniest of movements that would have resulted in her putting her hands behind her back, like that little girl in the photo.

The impact of her unconscious movement had been powerful. He'd been overwhelmed by the conviction that he couldn't let her draw back. He couldn't let her give in to that fear of rejection.

Did she even realize she did that? He didn't know, and he was certainly the last person who ought to be taking responsibility for her happiness.

"Link, it's beautiful."

He looked at her, enjoying her reaction to the room.

He'd forgotten how impressed people were the first time they came in, overwhelmed by the wall of glass looking out over the lake, the timbered walls, the immense fireplace. Annie's eyes were as bright as the candle flames that sparkled on each round, white-linen-covered table.

He covered her hand with his. "This isn't going to be hard," he said softly. "Just enjoy yourself."

It wasn't going to be hard for him, anyway, to show everyone they were a couple—not with the taste of her lips still on his.

"Is there likely to be a soul here that I know besides you?"

"Jenna and Pete ought to be around somewhere. They're saving us seats at their table." He turned to search the room for them. Instead, he found himself face-to-face with Frank and Julia.

"Link." Frank didn't offer to shake hands with him. "Annie." He gave her a stiff nod. "I didn't expect to see the two of you here."

"We wouldn't dream of missing the dinner," he said smoothly. He slid his arm around Annie's waist. "After all, this is the first chance I've had to introduce my bride to the rest of the business community."

"Of course." Frank smiled, recovering his balance. "You spend so much time out at the project that I don't think of you as part of the Downtown Business Association."

"You don't build houses by sitting in an office." *Or at least, I don't.* What Frank would do, if he took over Conrad and Morgan, was anyone's guess. But that wasn't going to happen. He wouldn't let it.

Frank's smile didn't falter. "I don't think a CEO has to get his hands dirty in order to run a company."

He resisted the urge to retort that Frank had never done enough work to know what it meant to get his hands dirty. But their cause wouldn't be served by getting into an argument with Frank in a public place.

He felt Annie's tension through the hand he'd rested on her waist. She was probably holding her breath, worrying about what he'd say next.

"Not everyone would agree with that," he said easily. "But you're entitled to your opinion."

"You might be surprised at the number of people who agree with me." Frank slid the dart in with a smile.

He felt Annie tremble, and anger surged through him. "If you think—"

Annie grabbed his hand. "Maybe we'd better find our seats, Link."

"Yes, of course." He tamped down his anger with an effort. He wasn't going to let Frank goad him, remember? He nodded to the two of them. "We'll see you later, I'm sure."

Julia, her mannequin's smile perfectly in place, turned away as if she hadn't heard. Frank gave him a look that set alarm bells ringing—the kind of look the cat might give the canary just before he pounced. Frank was just a little too pleased with himself, and that couldn't be good.

He steered Annie across the room. He must be catching some of her jitters. He and Annie were going to go into that custody suit and win. He wouldn't even imagine any other outcome.

Annie looked up at him, her brown eyes dark with worry. "What's wrong?"

"Nothing." He drew her a little closer. "Nothing at all is wrong." He hoped.

She studied his face for a moment. It must have been convincing, because she nodded.

"All right."

"There's Jenna and Pete." He gestured toward a table near the fireplace and held her hand firmly in his as they moved toward it.

They wanted everyone to see them as happily married. And he wanted her to feel secure.

But he knew he was kidding himself if he tried to believe that was the only reason he wanted Annie near him.

By the time dinner was over and the dancing had started, Annie was beginning to relax. This evening was going better than she'd have thought possible a few hours earlier.

Jenna and her husband, Pete, had been welcoming, introducing them to several other couples. No one had betrayed, by word or glance, that they thought there was anything odd about her and Link's sudden marriage. If anything, she'd had a sense of support, even belonging, that had made her glad she'd come.

How much of that sense of belonging had come from Link's solid presence next to her—from his easy smiles and light touches? He'd made her feel as if this were real.

Now, dancing close in his arms, she could almost believe it. The music and the soft murmur of voices formed the background. In the foreground was the strength of Link's arm around her, the warmth of his hand against her back, the touch of his breath across her cheek.

Did she dare let herself believe that a real relationship was possible between them? She squeezed his shoulder.

He tilted his head back, looking at her with a lazy smile that was only a few inches from her lips. "What was that for? Did you think I was falling asleep?"

"Just making sure this is real." She felt herself flush. She was probably giving herself away again, but if Link didn't know by now that she had feelings for him, he must be blind and deaf.

"It's real," he said softly against her ear. "I hope you're enjoying it, because I am."

She didn't want to think or analyze. She just wanted to be here, in this moment, with him.

The music ended. She didn't feel as if she could take the step that would put them apart.

"I don't want to go back to the table just now," he murmured. "Let's take a walk."

She nodded.

Holding her hand, Link led the way through the

crowd with such single-minded determination that it seemed to part in front of him. In a moment they were in the hallway, the sounds of the party muting behind them.

"This way." He walked quickly around the corner, away from the lobby. They passed a row of faded portraits on the wall, and he led her through another doorway.

The quiet room had low bookshelves running all the way around under the windows, a corner fireplace and a set of high-backed chairs facing the fire. It looked like the library in an English country house.

The only trouble was that it was already occupied. An elderly gentleman rose from one of the leather chairs at their entrance.

"Link." He held out his hand. "It's good to see you taking an evening off work."

Link's face softened, and he drew her forward. "Annie, I don't think you've met Doc Adams yet. Doc is one of our board members."

She extended her hand. "It's very nice to meet you, sir."

She found herself scrutinized by a pair of the shrewdest blue eyes she'd ever seen. Doc Adams had a dropping white mustache and bushy white hair, irresistibly reminding her of Samuel Clemens.

He let out a bark of laughter. "If a pretty girl calls me 'sir,' I must be even older than I think. Call me Doc, like everyone else."

"Doc," she corrected. She'd like to resent the man

for interrupting her quiet moment with Link, but his good humor was contagious. Even Link seemed relaxed in his presence.

"I was hoping I'd see you tonight, son." He put his hand on Link's shoulder. "Tell me, what's this board meeting going to be about?"

Link stared at him blankly. "Board meeting?"

Doc's bushy white brows lifted. "So you don't know about it. I wondered if that was the case—why I wanted to be sure and talk with you."

"I don't understand." Link's frown would frighten a lesser man. "We don't have a board meeting scheduled."

"We do now. Frank called one—we all got the notification today. For Tuesday afternoon."

"Tuesday?" Annie couldn't stop the question. "But we have the custody hearing on Wednesday morning." She looked at Link, knowing her apprehension must be written on her face.

Link's face had tightened to a mask. "What's on the agenda for the meeting?"

Doc shrugged. "Didn't say. I hoped you'd know. When I asked Frank, he'd only say it was a matter 'crucial to the future of the company.'"

"No." Link said tersely. "I have no idea what Frank's up to."

But it can't be good. She finished the thought for him, tension crawling along her nerves. Frank *was* up to something. The timing couldn't be a coincidence.

"Well, forewarned is forearmed, I always say."

Doc clapped him on the shoulder again. "Don't worry about it, son. It'd take something pretty big to convince me you're not doing a good job."

"Thanks, Doc." Link managed a smile.

The old man glanced from Link's face to hers. "Guess I'll leave you two alone, so you can talk without a fifth wheel getting in the way."

"You don't need to—" Annie began, but he was already out the door.

Link looked as if he'd been hit by a falling beam.

"It'll be all right." She said the first thing that came to mind, then realized they were words she'd use if Marcy bumped her knee. They hardly applied here.

He stared at her as if she'd lost her mind. "There's nothing all right about it. Frank wouldn't call a board meeting for the day before the hearing unless he had some scheme in mind. It can't be good for us."

"But can't you insist he tell the board what it's about? Or say it has to be scheduled some other time?"

His lips drew tight. "According to our rules, any board member can call a meeting at any time he deems it necessary. That was just intended to bypass the necessity of formal meetings, but Frank knows he can do it."

She shivered in spite of the warmth of the fire. "There must be something you can do."

"I'll talk to the other board members." Link turned

toward the door and then looked back at her impatiently. "Well, aren't you coming?"

Her heart seemed to freeze. Link's grim face didn't look anything like that of the man who'd held her close and whispered in her ear. Their moment of intimacy might never have been.

She should have known… Everything else paled in comparison to a threat to the company. In Link's world, nothing else was that important, especially not her.

Chapter Thirteen

"Can't we just sit down and try to figure this out rationally?"

Annie frowned at Link, whose pacing threatened to wear a rut in the family room carpet. He'd been this way since they'd learned of Frank's latest machinations the previous night. It was a wonder he'd been able to sit still through worship that morning.

He stopped pacing long enough to return her frown. "Sitting and thinking isn't going to stop Frank. We have to do something."

Link's words reminded her of their quarrel when he'd first proposed marriage as a solution to their problems. The only way Link knew to deal with a difficult situation was to charge right at it.

"Wearing a hole in the rug won't stop him, either. We can't take action unless we know what to do."

He stalked to the sofa and sat down, folding his arms. "Okay. Talk."

If she'd dreamed, even for a moment, that they could return to what they'd felt when they were dancing the night before, it was time to give up that dream. Link had apparently turned his feelings off as easily as flipping a switch.

"All right." Focus on the problem at hand—that was all she could do now. "We agree that the timing of this meeting Frank wants can't be coincidental. So what could he possibly hope to achieve at the board meeting that might impact the custody hearing?"

Link still frowned, but at least now the frown was directed not at her but at the situation.

"I wish I knew. I've talked to all three of the other board members. They claim Frank didn't tell them why he wanted a meeting."

"Do you believe them?"

He seemed to be assessing that. "I believe they're telling the truth as far as it goes. I suppose it's possible one of them—Frank's great-uncle, probably—might have some hint about what's on Frank's mind, but if so, nobody's talking."

They couldn't force the three elderly men to cooperate with them. The board members were even less likely to talk with her, a stranger, than with Link.

"Let's look at it from a different angle. What sort of thing would make any board member call an unexpected meeting? Has this ever happened before?"

"No." He answered the second question first, then

leaned forward. "They've been very much silent partners up until now." He held out one hand, palm up, as if the board sat there. "For the most part, they invested not so much because they were interested in the project as because they wanted to help Davis. They've never really shown much interest in the day-to-day running of the business."

"Except Frank. You said he'd been poking around the office and showing up at the site. What could he hope to find?"

His response was prompt. "Something to use against me."

"Like what? What could he possibly bring to the board that would turn them against you?"

"How do I know?" He flung his hand out in an angry gesture. "You'd have to see inside Frank's twisted reasoning to understand that."

She caught his hand and gripped it firmly, trying to ignore the pleasure it gave her to touch him. "That's not what I mean. If you could imagine something totally off base that would affect the board that way, what would it be?"

"Imagine?" He lifted one eyebrow, the faintest glimmer of amusement in his face for the first time since the previous night. "Is that really how accountants work? Imagining? You're not telling me Annie Gideon ever works on gut instinct, are you?"

Link's use of her maiden name took her aback for an instant. Odd, that she could have become used to being Annie Morgan so quickly. She forced herself to concentrate on his question.

"I know it shocks you, but sometimes that happens. For instance, I might get a sense that a client isn't telling me everything. Then I do have to use my imagination to come up with the right questions to ask. Otherwise, the auditor could look like a fool in an investigation."

He nodded, and she realized he was taking her seriously, at least for the moment.

"I get it." His frown deepened. "I suppose, if Frank could find evidence that I'd been diverting company funds or failing to pay in social security, they'd lose confidence in me pretty fast. But he can't, because I haven't."

"Davis did most of the bookkeeping—"

"If you can imagine Davis doing anything underhanded to endanger the company, you ought to be writing for the movies. He'd never do such a thing."

"I know that. I just meant that there might be something in the records that Frank hopes to distort." She was feeling her way, trying without much success to imagine herself in Frank's shoes.

"If there is, you'll have to find it. I wouldn't know what to look for."

Link surged to his feet, his supply of patience obviously at an end. But he didn't start pacing again He went to the closet and grabbed his windbreaker.

"Where are you going?"

He jammed his arms into the jacket sleeves.

"Look, I can't sit around talking any longer. Speculating isn't helping. I'm going out to the site."

Before she could formulate an argument, he'd stalked out of the house.

Lord, what am I going to do? The prayer that had been so often on her lips came again. *Link's so impatient. He can't see beyond this threat to the company. He's not even thinking about how it might affect our case.*

That was what frightened her even more than Frank's efforts, she realized. She was afraid that Link might, in his need to take action, do something that could be used against them.

We took vows to be one in Your sight, Father. Instead we're both running in opposite directions, trying to protect ourselves.

They weren't a team any longer. There had been moments in the past weeks when she'd thought they were—moments the night before when she'd dared to hope they'd become more than just two people whose goals coincided.

She'd intended to ask God to guide Link, but they both needed guidance right now, desperately. She bowed her head, holding both herself and Link up for God's direction. She listened, trying to discern an answer.

The words that floated up to the surface of her mind came in the pastor's voice. In their brief wedding ceremony in his office, Garth had talked about the process of two people becoming one. She'd been numb with grief and shock at the time, but somehow she'd stored away his words. He'd told them that the concept of two becoming one in marriage didn't mean that they should think or act alike. Instead they should complement each other, each filling in what the other lacked.

Link had said he wouldn't know what to look for in the company files. But she might.

She glanced at the clock. Marcy would probably sleep another hour. That was time enough to make a start. She went to the cabinet and pulled out her laptop. All the files from the office were on her computer.

Link didn't believe she could do anything to help. Maybe she couldn't, but she had to try.

She'd just have to trust that God would give her the wisdom to see what she needed to see.

Link checked the bracing on one rafter, then moved on to the next. Monday morning was half over, and he still didn't have any better idea of what Frank was planning.

He'd made a point of talking casually to each of the men this morning. His comments had been met with blank stares. No one seemed to have any ideas or even to have heard any rumors. Whatever Frank was doing, he was keeping it quiet, which was harder than one might think in a town like Lakeview.

When he'd come back to the house Sunday evening, a little embarrassed over rushing off half cocked, he'd found Annie dividing her attention between Marcy and the computer. She'd spent the afternoon working painstakingly through the company records, and she continued to do so long after they'd put Marcy to bed for the night.

He didn't think she was going to find anything. Frank was too clever to leave any obvious clues.

He pounded an additional nail into place with more force than was warranted. A little physical labor might help him think. Or at least take out his frustrations.

He had to admire Annie's persistence. Admire? He forced himself to look at his feelings. He cared for her, more deeply than he'd have thought possible a month ago. She amused him, annoyed him, made him question what he believed about himself. She drove him to distraction with her attention to details and to tenderness with her fears.

The truth stood out, plain enough to see. He knew what he wanted.

He wanted to make this marriage real. He wanted to go home every night to his wife and child, wanted to sleep every night with Annie beside him, wanted to wake up every morning with her face the first thing he saw.

For a while, on Saturday night, he'd been on the verge of telling her. Then the news of Frank's plotting had driven everything else from his mind. How could he possibly talk to Annie about his feelings when both of them were strained to the limit? But then, how could he keep quiet about it?

Maybe they'd both be better off bringing it out in the open before the custody hearing. If Annie returned his feelings—

The sound of a car on the gravel below distracted him. He looked over the edge of the roof to see Frank's black Porsche pull to a stop.

His muscles knotted. Somehow he didn't think Frank was here on a casual visit. Maybe he was finally going to get some answers.

He walked to the ladder, then climbed down, not hurrying. Frank had come to him. He wouldn't make the strategic mistake of seeming too desperate.

At the bottom, he propped an elbow on the ladder and waited.

Frank got out of the car, stood for a moment, then sauntered toward him with a slightly annoyed look on his face. He stopped at the edge of the gravel and nodded toward his polished shoes.

"I'm not exactly dressed for the site. How about coming over here?"

He considered offering Frank a hard hat, then decided not to push it. Instead, he took a long step over the drainage ditch and joined him.

"What brings you out here today?"

Frank smiled. "Just thought I'd like to take a look at what my money is doing."

"Your ten percent, you mean?"

The smile took on an edge. "You and Davis were happy enough to get my ten percent, as I recall."

"What do you want, Frank?" Well, so much for strategy, or anything else that involved patience. He didn't have it in him. "We both know you didn't come out here to look around."

Frank looked at him for a moment, as if deciding how much he intended to say. Then he shrugged. "Well, since you want to be blunt, I'll come to the point."

"Good idea. Why don't you tell me what the purpose is for the board meeting you called for tomorrow?"

Frank lifted an eyebrow. "According to the bylaws, I don't have to reveal that until the meeting." His smile was annoyingly self-satisfied. "So we'll let that be a surprise. If there is a board meeting."

"If?" The word alerted him. Frank was here to offer a deal.

"No sense dragging dirty linen out into the open. We can settle all this easily—keep it in the family, so to speak."

"You and I aren't family."

"No, but Marcy and I are."

The reminder struck him in the heart. He wasn't related to Marcy, and any standing he had was because of his marriage to Annie.

"So?" He wasn't about to let Frank see that his words bothered him.

"So it might be best for all concerned if we didn't

have to go through with things like board meetings and custody hearings.''

''Cut to the chase, Frank. What do you want?''

''Shall we make a deal? You and Annie want custody of Marcy. I want control of the company.'' He seemed to balance the two options in his manicured hands. ''You give me what I want, and I'll give you what you want.''

A chill gripped the back of Link's neck. Frank must be very sure of himself to make an offer like that.

He couldn't let that rattle him. ''You're taking a risk here, aren't you? What if Mrs. Bradshaw or the judge heard you offering to trade Marcy for control of the company?''

''Nobody will hear me. This is just between us. And, as advertisers like to say, it's a one-time offer. Save yourself and Annie a great deal of trouble and say yes now.''

Annie. His heart twisted. What would Annie think if she heard this?

Lord, this can't be right, can it? I can't give up everything I've worked for all these years.

That was the bottom line for him. He wouldn't give up, and he wouldn't give in, not without a fight.

''Sorry, Frank.'' He'd enjoy the look on the other man's face if this situation weren't so serious. So Frank had really thought he'd surrender that easily, had he? ''I don't feel like making a deal. I'll take my chances with the board and with the judge.''

Frank's mouth tightened. ''Have it your way.'' He

stalked back toward his car, flinging out his hand in a gesture toward the project. "When you lose everything, remember I made the offer."

Link stood watching as the small car flew out of the parking area, spraying gravel. What he wanted to do was jump in his truck and head straight for Annie to talk this over with her.

But he wouldn't. Annie was stressed enough. She didn't need anything else to upset her just before the custody hearing.

And that meant he wouldn't be telling her his feelings, either. He couldn't take the risk of tipping the precarious balance both of them were trying to maintain.

He'd wait until after the hearing. They'd win. He had to believe that.

And then he'd ask her to stay.

"More coffee?" Annie held the pot poised over Link's mug at breakfast on Tuesday morning. He shook his head, not glancing up from the day's newspaper.

Annie looked automatically at the calendar on the kitchen corkboard. *Tuesday morning.* Roughly six hours until the board meeting, and they had no weapon with which to fight Frank.

Twenty-four hours, more or less, until the custody hearing, and they still didn't know what Mrs. Bradshaw's recommendation would be. Or whether the judge would let the social worker's report make the decision for her, even if it was favorable.

"At least Chet seemed positive." She didn't realize she'd spoken aloud until Link glanced up at her.

He nodded. "He feels we're as ready as anyone can possibly be."

They'd met with the attorney on the previous afternoon, talking over their strategy, such as it was. All they could do was tell the truth. Their feelings hadn't changed, and they believed Marcy was better off with them.

Unspoken had been Link's obvious worry over the board meeting. He might, of course, have discussed that with Chet privately.

She studied Link's averted face. If he had, he wasn't sharing that with her. He'd closed all the doors she'd thought were beginning to crack open to her.

Because he was trying to protect her? Or because he didn't want her to intrude? Either way, the result was the same. He'd shut her out.

There was nothing she could do about it. She glanced down at the plain gold band on her finger. Marriage—the kind of marriage they had, at any rate—didn't mean she could force him to confide in her.

He put the paper down and looked at her, eyes shadowed. "Are you taking Marcy to play group this morning?"

"I haven't decided. Maybe I ought to spend the time digging through the company records." She didn't need to say she'd been unsuccessful so far. That was obvious.

He shook his head, shoving his chair back from the table. "I wouldn't bother."

She felt a flicker of anger. "Because you think I can't find anything."

"No." He touched her shoulder lightly, then took his hand away. "Because I don't think there's anything to find. Whatever Frank's up to, he won't have left any traces." His hand bunched into a fist, and he seemed unaware of that. "I was just remembering Chet's advice—to keep things as normal as possible."

"All right." She stood, too. He was leaving, and the barricades he'd erected between them made her feel bereft and alone. "We'll go to play group." She glanced at Marcy, contentedly chewing on a toast crust in her high chair. "Marcy will like that."

He gave a curt nod. "Good. I'd better get going, then. I want to get in a few hours' work at the site before the meeting."

He started toward the door, and she had to force herself not to follow. For her to look needy didn't help either of them.

Link reached the door, jacket in hand. He paused, head down, as if debating something. Then he spun, stalked back across the room, and kissed her hard and fast.

"It'll be all right." His hands were tight on her arms. "It has to be."

Before she could respond, he'd turned away and was gone.

Chapter Fourteen

Annie lifted her hands from the piano keys, smiling at the enthusiastic clapping of her small audience.

"More songs, more songs!" Jenna's two-year-old pounded on the piano bench, his face wreathed in smiles.

"Not just now." Jenna swooped on him, picking him up. "We'll talk Ms. Annie into more songs later. Who wants a bagel?"

The toddlers swarmed after her to the kitchen, followed by mothers. Linda paused to give Annie a quick hug.

"That was great! You have to promise to play every time. The kids loved it."

She slid off the piano bench. "As long as you don't expect anything more complicated, I'll be happy to." *If I'm here. If we get custody of Marcy. If—*

No, she wouldn't let herself obsess about that now. She'd concentrate on keeping things normal.

Normal had changed so much in the past month. She followed Marcy into the kitchen and broke off a piece of bagel for her. Who would have believed she'd be a part of this laughing, chattering group? Who'd have believed she'd feel comfortable enough with them to let her fingers fumble over the piano keys?

She'd changed. Hard as it was to believe anything good had come out of a terrible tragedy, she'd become a different person as a result of her loss—better, more open, more loving.

Please, Lord, don't let me lose this.

She picked up Marcy and slid onto a chair at the kitchen table with the baby on her lap. "Jenna, this is lovely."

"Bagels and fruit. Everyone's favorite." Jenna sat down next to her. "Listen, guys. I was thinking we ought to go on another outing with the kids before the weather turns cold."

Everyone had an opinion on that, it seemed. Ideas bounced around the table.

Annie's throat tightened suddenly. They were including her in their plans, assuming nothing would go wrong. If only…

She concentrated on fixing another piece of bagel for Marcy. She wouldn't let herself dream of that. She couldn't. Link had closed the door.

But he'd kissed her. Her lips seemed to warm with the memory. That meant something, didn't it?

"...so, anyway, I said to the teller, 'I've been banking here for ten years. The least you could do is let me know I was overdrawn.'"

Jenna had obviously begun telling a story while she was thinking about Link.

"Then I had to track down all the places my checks had bounced. I felt like a deadbeat."

Annie laughed along with everyone else at Jenna's woeful expression, knowing that Jenna cheerfully confessed her total inability to keep her checkbook balanced.

Somehow, in the midst of the laughter, an idea trickled into her mind. She looked at it cautiously. No, that couldn't be the answer. That was too simple.

Simple, but very effective. Excitement jumped along her nerves like lightning. Every auditor knew that the simplest tricks could sometimes be the hardest to spot.

"Annie?" Jenna nudged her. "You look as if you're a million miles away. What is it?"

"An idea." An idea that might make a difference, if she was right. "Jenna, would you mind watching Marcy for a few hours? There's something I have to do, right away."

Jenna nodded. "No problem. The kids will enjoy it. Take all the time you need."

She glanced at her watch. Only two hours until the meeting. She wouldn't need all that much time.

Please, Lord, guide me to the answers. Let me find the truth before it's too late.

Annie hurried across the square, red and gold leaves thrust by the wind sweeping along with her. She'd considered driving, but all of the places she'd needed to reach were situated in the blocks around the square—everything important in Lakeview centered there.

She crossed the street, her gaze darting ahead to search for the number of Harvey Ward's real estate office. The board meeting was to be held there, in his conference room.

She glanced at her watch. She should still have a few minutes to spare, as long as they hadn't started early. Even with Vera's help, it had taken more time than she'd anticipated to find what she needed.

Then she'd rushed to the bank. She had to bring back documentation to satisfy the board.

There it was—another redbrick building, like most of the buildings around the square. She hurried up the steps, asked the receptionist for the conference room, and reached the hallway to see Link about to open the door.

"Link." She said his name, trying to catch her breath and smooth down wind-ruffled hair. "Just a minute."

His glance said he was so preoccupied with the challenge ahead that he barely realized she was there. She caught his wrist, feeling the strong pulse under his skin. "This can't wait. I found it. I know what Frank's up to with the board."

For an instant he just stared at her, as if not sure he'd heard her right. Then he pulled her along the hall to where it ended at a window looking onto a brick wall next door. He drew her close.

"What are you talking about? What did you find?" His voice was low and urgent.

"It was the loan payment." She lowered her voice, too, glancing down the hallway to be sure the door to the conference room was closed. "The payment that should have been made this month to the bank. It was never made."

Link's level brows drew down. "That's impossible. Even without Davis, one of us would have paid it."

"I talked to Vera. The only thing she can think is that in the confusion after Davis died, you each thought the other had taken care of it."

"But the accounts—"

"The accounts indicate that it was paid," she said levelly. "But Vera didn't. And you didn't."

"Someone tampered with the records." His jaw tightened, and a vein throbbed at his temple. "I guess we both know who that was."

"There's no way of proving it," she said quickly. "Link, I know you want to accuse him, but there's no proof. If he wants to act as if it was all a mistake—"

"You want me to let him save face after what he's done." Link didn't look as if that were within the realm of possibility.

"I want you not to get into a public fight with him if you can help it." She'd thought about this as she raced from the office to the bank to the meeting. "The hearing's tomorrow, remember? Surely it's better not to give people anything to gossip about at this point."

"If we could prove he tampered with the files, it would tell against him."

"But we can't." She put her hand on his arm. It was as rigid as stone. "Please, Link."

"All right," he said abruptly. "We'll do it your way, Annie."

"Good." She took a breath. *Good.* "Vera and I made the payment and paid the late charges. Here's the receipt from the bank."

He took it, then faced the conference room, his face as taut and determined as that of a crusader going into battle. "I have to get in there."

"Yes." She let her hand drop.

Mentally, Link was already in the room, already fighting his private war with Frank. At some point, he'd stop and think, realize what she'd done, probably be grateful.

But right now, he didn't have time for her or anything else. Saving his company was the only thing on his mind. She'd given him the ammunition he needed to win this round. She'd have to be content with that.

Link put the bank receipt in the center of the polished walnut table, resisting the impulse to throw it in Frank's smug face. Annie wouldn't like it if he did that.

"I'm afraid you're mistaken, Frank. The loan payment has been made."

He kept his gaze fixed on Frank's face as Frank snatched up the receipt, but he was aware of the current running around the table. Doc Adams looked gratified, as if his faith in Link hadn't been misplaced. Harvey Ward glanced at his watch, as if ready for another meeting. Delbert Conrad, Davis's uncle and the oldest board member, just looked relieved. He'd been devoted to Davis, but too fragile to be up for a battle.

They hadn't wanted to believe Frank was right in his claim that Link's mismanagement had put their investment in jeopardy. Even in the midst of his concentration on Frank, he was glad of that. They had wanted to trust him.

If he hadn't been able to produce the proof of payment? The board members wouldn't have liked it, but they'd have been too worried about their own liability to do anything else. They'd have voted for the motion Frank had introduced, removing Link and installing Frank as president and chairman of the board.

Frank would have had the power he wanted without waiting for his chance to control Marcy's inheritance. And he'd undoubtedly thought that discrediting Link would help him at the custody hearing.

Frank seemed to be struggling to control his expression. "I note the payment was late. We can't afford—"

"Now, Frank." Doc Adams's voice held a note of authority. "It's hardly an issue this time. We all realize it must have been difficult this month." He pinned Link with a determined gaze. "I assume that is the case, isn't it?"

Apparently Doc Adams held the same view Annie did. *Don't make public waves.*

"It looks that way. Somehow the ledger had been marked 'paid.' I suppose Vera and I each assumed the other had made the payment. There's no way of knowing how it became erroneously marked."

Annie would be proud of his ability to think this through rationally instead of acting on his gut instinct. Maybe he was learning that from her. Harvey and Delbert were both nodding, as if his explanation made perfect sense to them.

Annie. He'd been so caught up in this battle, he'd never even thanked her. More to the point, he hadn't admitted to her that he'd been wrong. She *had* found the answer. Her tenacity and passion for detail had saved him.

"Well." Frank cleared his throat. "I'm glad, in that event, that this has all been straightened out. I certainly didn't want to be the one to bring it up."

No one sitting around the table believed him, of course, but they'd all pretend they did.

"Suppose we adjourn this meeting," Doc said. "I don't think we can accomplish anything else here."

There was a general chorus of relieved agreement, and people began getting up. Frank was the first one to the door. He paused just long enough to give Link a look of pure dislike, and then he left.

Doc waited until the other men had gone out, then he put his hand on Link's arm. "Looks as if you came out ahead of him this time, son."

He took a deep breath, trying to release some of the adrenaline that had carried him through the past hour. "Thanks to your early warning, Doc."

Doc waved a hand. "All I did was mention the meeting. You figured out how to handle it."

"Actually, I didn't." For the first time in days he felt like smiling. "Annie did that. If it hadn't been for her, I'd have been knocked flat by Frank's accusation, and he'd be sitting at the head of the table by now."

"Sounds as if she's a smart young woman."

"She is." She was much more than that.

Doc glanced at the chair placed at the head of the polished table. "You know, that is what Frank wanted. The trappings of success—the title, the power." He shook his head. "I knew both those boys from the time they were born. Davis, even with his problems, always had good stuff inside. But all Frank ever cared about was what he looked like to the world."

Doc made it sound like an epitaph. His words had an eerie similarity to the verse he'd quoted to Annie.

There was something else strange about it. Those

were things that *he* wanted. They were the things that he felt spelled acceptance.

He rejected the thought as soon as it formed. He wasn't like Frank.

"Well, I'd best be on my way home." Doc clapped him on the shoulder again. "Good luck to the two of you tomorrow. You ready for that hearing?"

"As ready as we can be, I guess. Thanks, Doc."

He walked out slowly, fitting his steps to those of the older man. Doc had been around a long time. He knew most of what there was to know about humanity. He'd sized Frank up pretty thoroughly.

Did he realize he'd held a mirror up to Link, as well? Maybe, maybe not. Either way, Link was going to have trouble not thinking about it.

It wasn't wrong to want to achieve his goals. He'd worked long and hard to build the company, to develop friendships, to secure a place in the community.

He had a good facade now. No one would guess he'd been one of the throwaway kids.

Trouble was, Doc's words had made him wonder just exactly what kind of man he was beneath that facade.

Annie found herself glancing out the window for the twentieth time. Not that she was watching for Link, but it was a relief to see his truck pull into the driveway.

He got out of the truck and stood for a moment, his tall figure outlined against it. Then he walked slowly toward the house, looking down, seemingly in thought.

Her heart seemed to stop. Link didn't look as if he were celebrating. The meeting—

She threw the door open, then grabbed Marcy as she bolted straight for it.

"What is it? What's wrong? Did Frank have something else besides the bank payment?"

Link held up his hands to hold off her questions. "No, not at all. He was dumbfounded."

Marcy, thwarted from getting outside, decided to climb Link's pants leg instead. He lifted her in his arms, tickling her cheek.

"Then, why did you look so upset?"

He shook his head, shrugging out of his jacket without putting Marcy down. "Sorry. I was just thinking. I should have called you, but it was getting so late I thought I might as well come home and tell you."

The tension that had gripped her at the sight of him eased. But something was still wrong. He didn't act like a man who'd just won a battle.

"How did Frank react? What did the board members say? Do I have to pry it out of you?"

His face relaxed then, his smile reaching his eyes. "Sorry. Am I being annoying?"

"Just a little."

"Frank brought it up right away—made a motion, in fact, that since I'd proved to be 'fiscally irresponsible,' he should replace me."

He sat on the sofa, extending his hand to pull her down beside him. Marcy, not content to sit still, wiggled her way down and ran to her toy cabinet.

"How did the board respond?" If the board had turned against Link easily, that might account for his attitude. She knew how he valued their good opinion, especially Doc's.

He shrugged. "They wanted to give me the benefit of the doubt, I think. But with Frank pushing them and the statement from the bank that we were behind in our payments, he had a good argument."

"Until you produced today's receipt."

"The receipt you brought me." He squeezed her hand. "After you left, I realized I hadn't even thanked you. You saved me today, Annie. You've got to be the smartest accountant in the world. How did you get onto it?"

That surprised a laugh out of her. "Not by being a smart accountant, as a matter of fact," she said, and she told him about Jenna's experience.

"And that made you think of it?" He held her hand close, and the admiration in his eyes made her heart thump.

"It made me start thinking about how the board would react if something like that happened." She made an effort to sound professional. "At first I thought of the company's account being overdrawn, but that wasn't the case. Then I thought about the loan payment." She relived those moments in the office. "Vera insisted the payment had been recorded, but my instinct told me to check with the bank. And there it was."

"You told me once that a good auditor relied on instinct. If you hadn't this time..." His eyes darkened.

"I did, so all's well that ends well." A shiver ran down her back in spite of the warm clasp of his hand. "If Frank had won today, we'd have gone into the hearing tomorrow with a pretty heavy strike against us."

She looked at Marcy, busy pulling everything out of her toy box. They could have lost her. They still could.

"He'd have presented me as a financial failure who wasn't taking proper care of Marcy's inheritance." Link's jaw tightened. "He wouldn't have stopped at becoming chairman of the board. He still wants control of Marcy's inheritance, and I almost gave him the weapon he needed to take it."

"It wasn't your fault." That must be what was bothering him—the thought that he'd put Marcy's custody in jeopardy. "You couldn't have been expected to see the problem. I must have looked over those accounts a half dozen times without realizing anything was wrong."

"I should have double-checked on the payment. I knew when it was due." He seemed determined to blame himself.

"You were trying to do everything yourself—your

own work and Davis's, too. Nobody could do all that without missing something.''

''This was a pretty big something, Annie.''

''You wouldn't have missed it, if someone hadn't altered the records.'' She wanted to smooth away the frown lines on his forehead with her fingertips, but she didn't quite dare. ''I wish we could pin it on him, but I'm afraid it's impossible. You didn't—''

''No, I didn't start a public fight with him.'' His tone was gently teasing. ''I was tempted, but I knew you wouldn't like it.''

The look in his eyes flustered her. ''Well, it—it's not just me,'' she said hurriedly. ''I mean, we both agreed we didn't want to give people anything bad to talk about on the day before the hearing.''

''Right.'' He squeezed her hand. ''Tell you what. Let's give people something nice to talk about, instead. I'll get changed, and then I'll take my two best girls out for dinner. Okay?''

''That sounds lovely. What do you think, Marcy? Want to go out to eat?''

Marcy looked up, holding her toy telephone to her ear, and let out a string of babble that might have meant anything.

''I think she agrees.'' Link stood. ''Be ready in a few minutes. You pick the place.''

He touched her cheek, very lightly, and then turned and jogged up the stairs. Marcy let out a wail and started after him. Annie grabbed her.

''Come on, sweetheart. Let's get you changed, too.

Then Link and Nan and Marcy will all go out to dinner.''

She lifted the baby, holding her close for a moment. Link didn't fool her. He'd suggested this dinner out as a way of keeping her mind off what tomorrow would bring.

Chapter Fifteen

"We'll just take a few minutes to talk before we go over to the courthouse," Chet said as he waved them toward the chairs in his office the next morning.

Annie held Marcy on her lap, her arms close around the child as if she never intended to let go. Link knew how she felt. He'd had trouble saying good-night to Marcy the night before, trouble squashing the fear that that might be the last time he'd do it.

"Tell us honestly." Annie's face was pale. "What are our chances?"

Chet folded his hands together on his desk. "Honestly? It's hard to say. I think they're very good, but custody is never a sure thing." He glanced at Link. "I'll tell you one thing—your chances would have been a lot worse if Frank had won control of the company yesterday. That whisper of financial irresponsibility would have dogged you. Even if you eventually could have straightened it out, it might have been too late.''

"Frank timed it well.'' With an effort, Link kept his voice even. "If not for Annie, I would have lost.''

A glow brightened Annie's cheeks at his words.

"It's a shame you can't prove Frank manipulated the records. I'd have enjoyed bringing that up at the hearing.'' Chet turned his pen over and over on the desk blotter. "As it is, we're relying on the social worker's report, coupled with the fact that the judge gave you initial custody.'' He looked searchingly at Annie. "Mrs. Bradshaw didn't give you any hint as to her recommendation?''

Annie shook her head, and the helplessness in her eyes wrung Link's heart. If he could find anything that would help her...

Frank's offer to him. Maybe Chet could see a way to bring that in.

"There is one other thing.'' He glanced at Annie. "I didn't tell you because I didn't want to worry you. But Frank came out to the site on Monday. He made me an offer.''

"What kind of offer?'' Chet leaned forward, his pen poised over a legal pad.

"He offered to make a trade with us. We could forget both the board meeting and the custody hearing. They'd give us custody of Marcy if I gave him control of the company.''

He heard Annie's indrawn, strangled breath, but he focused on Chet's face. "Can we use it?"

Chet frowned. "I don't suppose anyone else heard him say it."

"No." Frank hadn't been dumb enough to risk that. "The men probably saw us talking, but no one was close enough to hear what was said."

"Too bad. It's just the sort of thing we need, but without any corroboration, we don't dare bring it up." Chet stood, glancing at his watch. "Let me just check on something with my secretary, and then we'll be ready to go."

When the door had closed behind him, Link turned to Annie. "Try not to worry too much. If—"

"Worry?" Annie's voice rose, and she made an obvious effort to control herself. "Of course I'm worried. I'm also angry. How could you turn down Frank's offer without even talking to me about it?"

"You were already upset about his calling the board meeting. I thought it would just make things worse to know he felt that confident."

She was shaking her head before he finished saying the words. "That's not why. You didn't tell me because you'd already made the decision for both of us."

Her anger sparked his. "What did you expect me to do? Turn the company over to Frank without a fight?"

"I expected you to consult me about something that affected Marcy's future."

She wrapped her arms around the baby as if protecting the child from him. Marcy, apparently sensing that something was wrong, looked up, her small face puckering.

How had things deteriorated between them so quickly? He tried for rationality. "Look, Annie, I was only trying to do what was best for everyone."

"And you were the one who got to decide what that best was." Her face was pale and set.

His determination hardened. "I knew what I had to do. I wasn't giving up the company without a fight. I thought you understood what it means to me."

For an instant, Doc's words from the day before echoed in his mind, and he pushed them away angrily. He wasn't like Frank.

"It means everything to you," she said flatly, all the emotion wiped from her voice and her face. "I should have realized that, shouldn't I?"

"This isn't just for me." Why didn't she see that? "This is for Davis, for Davis's child. I owe him my loyalty."

He'd thought she couldn't get any whiter, but she did. Her fingers were bloodless where they gripped each other around Marcy.

"Loyalty," she repeated. "Yes. Your loyalty was always to Davis and his family, wasn't it."

Never to me. She didn't say the words, but they echoed in the still air between them like a death knell.

Annie held Marcy against her chest as they walked out of the office, the baby's softness the only thing that kept her heart from breaking into pieces. It took a physical wrench to put Marcy into the stroller when they reached the sidewalk.

Link reached for the stroller handle. She turned away, pushing the stroller quickly along the sidewalk until she reached the corner. She didn't want him to touch the baby. She didn't want him to touch her. The shield she'd always depended upon to protect her heart was completely gone now, leaving her vulnerable and exposed.

The light changed, and they crossed to the square in silence. Her footsteps rustled through a path of fallen leaves, red and gold against the walk, a mute reminder of the time that had passed since they'd made this same trip a month ago.

They probably looked the same to an observer. But they weren't. Everything was different.

She took a fractured breath, the pain heavy in her chest. She loved him. She'd lost him. She wouldn't get over this so easily.

They reached the courthouse steps. She lifted Marcy from the stroller, ignoring the hand Link reached out to help.

Please, Lord. She tried to bring order to the chaos of her thoughts. *Lord, help me. In a few minutes we'll be in the hearing. They could take Marcy away from me. I have to get control of myself.*

She took a breath, then another. Chet held the door open for her, and she walked into the courthouse. All right. Slowly the pain receded to a dull throbbing. It would spring to life again later, and she'd have to deal with it then.

Now, she needed all her strength to cope with the hearing.

No, I need Your strength, Father. I don't have enough of my own. I put Marcy in Your hands.

Calmness settled over her. She would get through the hearing. Then, either way, she would get through the dissolution of the marriage that could never have been real, no matter how much she wanted it.

They rode up in the elevator, still silent, still strangers. As they moved out into the upstairs hallway, she saw Mrs. Bradshaw waiting for them. The woman stepped forward, her stern face softening in a smile when she looked at Marcy.

"The judge has asked me to watch Marcy during the hearing." She held out her hands. "Don't worry. I'll take good care of her."

Annie could almost imagine that was compassion in the woman's voice. Fear settled into her heart. Was Mrs. Bradshaw compassionate because she knew that her report had gone against them?

It took every bit of control she could muster to kiss Marcy and hand her to the social worker. Marcy, sensing tension, tried to cling to her.

"It's all right, sweetheart. You remember Mrs. Bradshaw. She's going to play with you for a bit."

Mollified, Marcy let herself be passed over. The woman nodded, then carried the baby quickly into a nearby room. The sound of the door closing was like a blow to Annie's heart.

"It's all right." Link repeated her words. "You'll have her back again before you know it."

She nodded. Her lips were too stiff to manage a smile. She turned to Chet. "I need a few minutes before we go in."

He glanced at his watch. "Go ahead. There's a women's lounge around the corner."

She walked quickly away, needing to be out of Link's sight for a few minutes at least. Her footsteps echoed on the tile floor.

She rounded the corner and nearly walked into Frank. Before she could turn away, he took her arm.

"You're just the person I wanted to see. I'd like a word before we go in."

"I don't think there's anything we have to say to each other." She tried to pull her arm free, but his grip held her in place.

"Oh, but there is." He smiled.

Frank smiles and smiles, and all the while... Fear shot through her.

She forced it away. That was ridiculous. What could Frank possibly do to her in a public place, with Link right around the corner?

She tried for a reasonable tone. "I'm sure we should let our lawyers do the talking for us. The judge will decide what's best."

"Wouldn't you rather settle this between us?"

It was an echo of Frank's offer to Link. All her defenses went up.

"I don't see how that's possible." She tried to free her arm. Why didn't someone else come along this end of the hallway?

"It's perfectly possible. Even easy. All I want is the company. I'm sure you know that."

"Yes." Her anger sparked. "It's too bad the judge can't hear you say so."

"You know I wouldn't be foolish enough to say this where anyone else would hear. Now, you're a bright young woman." For an instant his face darkened. "Bright enough to ferret out the truth about the loan payment, I imagine. I don't think Link did that on his own."

"You're not giving him enough credit." Even after what Link had done, she was still defending him.

He dismissed Link with a wave of his hand. "He doesn't matter. I'm making this offer to you. You make sure I get the company, and I'll guarantee you get custody of Marcy. Simple as that."

"It's too late. There's nothing I can do to make that happen."

"Of course there is. All you have to do is go into the hearing and admit to the judge that your marriage is a sham. That you only married Link to get custody of Marcy and control of the company. That's all."

She could only stare at him. "You must think I'm crazy. If I did that, the judge would grant custody to you."

"And as soon as Marcy's shares are in my hands, we'll turn her over to you. You can raise her as you see fit. We won't interfere, as long as I control her shares."

"You're asking me to trust you'd keep your end of the bargain. Why would I?" It was ridiculous even to be having this conversation. And yet she couldn't seem to stop her mind from looking at the possibility.

"Surely you don't think Julia and I really want to raise a child, do you? It was all I could do to convince Julia to pretend for a month. This way, we each get what we want. Everybody's happy."

"Everybody but Link."

"Link will survive. He'll still have his share of the company. He'll just have to report to me." Frank released her arm. "Think about it, but think fast. Once you've testified, the chance will be gone."

Once more, Annie found herself seated in the judge's chambers with Link on one side of her and Chet on the other. Once more, Judge Carstairs sat behind the massive mahogany desk. The huge desk might have been expected to dominate the book-lined room, but it didn't. Judge Carstairs did.

"All right, let's get started." The judge glanced at them. "We're keeping this informal, as I said. No one outside this room needs to know what happens here."

Annie was already cold, and the ominous words seemed to freeze her into immobility. She wanted to look at Link but she couldn't. He might see the temptation to betray him in her eyes.

He betrayed you, didn't he? The voice of temptation was soft in her ear. *If you play it safe, go along with Frank, you'll get Marcy. That's the only important thing.*

If she did that, how would she live with herself? If she lost Marcy—

No, that didn't bear thinking about.

Please, Lord. Panic filled her mind, disrupting the prayer.

"I already have the social worker's report." The judge lifted a manila folder from the desk blotter.

She raised her hand, seeming to silence a protest Frank's attorney was about to make. Annie felt Chet move slightly, as if he'd thought of speaking and changed his mind.

"I want to hear from all the participants, telling me in their own words why this little girl should be given into their care. The attorneys for each side can ask any questions that are pertinent." She glanced down at the report, then looked at Frank. "We'll begin with Mr. Lester."

An invisible hand tightened around Annie's throat. Was she beginning with the Lesters because the social worker had recommended them?

Frank looked startled, but seemed to regain his balance as he stood to be sworn in, then resumed his seat next to Julia. The judge nodded to him encouragingly.

"Well, Your Honor, the baby's father was my

cousin. We grew up together here in Lakeview. I'm a member of the board of his company. My wife and I have been married for eight years, we're lifelong residents of Lakeview, and we're fully prepared to provide Marcy with a stable, loving home.''

Liar. All you want is the company.

If only the judge had seen and heard what she had. But there was no way of proving anything. Chet had made it clear they could make no accusations they couldn't prove.

''Mrs. Lester?''

Then Julia was speaking, talking about how she'd always loved Marcy and what pleasure she'd taken in setting up a nursery just for her.

All the while she talked, Annie's fears bounced around and around in her brain. *Please, Lord.* The prayer was desperate. *Please show me what to do.*

''Mr. Longly, do you have any questions for either of the Lesters?''

''No, Your Honor.''

''Let's go to Mrs. Morgan, then.''

Suddenly she was being sworn in. *Last chance.* The words kept echoing in her mind. *This is your last chance.*

Judge Carstairs was looking at her, waiting for her to begin. Annie could feel the intensity of Frank's gaze on her face, as if he willed her to say what he wanted.

She swallowed, trying to find her voice. ''I love Marcy.'' As soon as the words were out, her tight throat eased. "My sister and I were very close. I was there when Marcy was born—I was the first person to hold her after Davis and Becca. I've been taking care of her since Becca's death, and I'm sure Becca would expect me to continue to do so."

She came to a halt, not sure she could say anything else. What else was there to say? She loved Marcy for herself, not for anything that came along with her.

"Ms. Marshall?" The judge recognized the Lesters' attorney.

"I have a few questions for Mrs. Morgan, Your Honor."

The judge nodded.

Annie braced herself. The woman was going to ask about their marriage. Frank was giving her the opportunity to take the deal he offered.

"Mrs. Morgan, isn't it a fact that you and Mr. Morgan only married in order to gain control of the child and her inheritance? Isn't it true that the two of you have no feelings for each other, and that this is simply a marriage of convenience, undertaken to fool the court?"

Chet was on his feet in an instant, objecting to the question, but Annie barely heard him.

All she could really focus on was her own heart, and suddenly she could do so more clearly than she had in her entire life.

She'd been telling herself that loving Marcy and being loved by the child was enough for her. But that was cheating. She'd longed all her life to be loved, but she'd never been willing to take the emotional risk needed to deserve it.

"Mrs. Morgan?" Judge Carstairs prompted her. "Will you answer the question?"

"Yes, Your Honor." It was suddenly very clear. No matter what Link had done, no matter what the future held for them, all she could do was tell the truth.

Father, give her the wisdom to see into my heart as clearly as You do.

"It's true that Link and I married when we did because it seemed best for Marcy." She said the words slowly and clearly, knowing she was laying her heart out for all to see. "But that doesn't mean we have no feelings for each other. I love my husband with all my heart."

There. It was done.

Chapter Sixteen

Link's breath caught and his heart seemed to twist. Annie—his Annie—had sat there and told the world that she loved him. Through a tumult of emotions, he could barely hear Chet arguing something with the opposing attorney. He couldn't seem to concentrate on that—on anything.

One thing stood clear in his mind. Annie wouldn't lie. She was telling the truth. She loved him.

Exultation swept through him, closely followed by a hard sock of reality. Annie might love him, but she still faulted him for making that decision without talking to her. She thought that meant his loyalty wasn't to her.

All of a sudden the answer that had always seemed right—that he'd done what he thought was best for all of them—didn't sound so right anymore. What had been so important that he had to make that decision without her?

He knew the answer to that. The company. He hadn't even considered the possibility of doing something that would affect his stake in the company.

Doc's words, when he'd talked about Frank, echoed in his mind again. Doc had held a mirror up to Link without even knowing it. In that mirror, Link saw a man consumed with the facade marked ''acceptance'' and ''success.''

It was time to call a halt to that. If God looked at his heart, he didn't want Him to find a hollow shell.

Annie had just done the hardest thing in the world for her to do. She'd opened her arms and taken the risk of offering love with no certainty that her gift would be welcomed.

If only he could talk to her—but he couldn't. Already he was being sworn in. All he could do was reach out and take her hand, not sure whether he was offering strength or asking for it.

''Would you like to say a few words, Mr. Morgan?''

''Yes, Your Honor.''

Annie had been willing to sacrifice her vulnerable heart. He knew what he had to sacrifice to make this right.

He cleared his throat. ''Your Honor, I still believe what I said the first time we met here. My wife loves Marcy more than anything. She's the best person to have custody of this little girl.''

He glanced at Frank, trying to overcome his dislike. "I realize that Frank, as Davis's cousin, feels that he has a claim on the child, too." He felt Annie's hand jerk in his. "So I'd like to propose a compromise."

He looked at Annie, hoping that she could read the love in his eyes. "I haven't had a chance to talk this over with my wife, and I'm sorry about that."

Annie squeezed his hand, as if encouraging him.

"What is this compromise, Mr. Morgan?" Judge Carstairs studied him, her expression giving nothing away.

He took a breath and murmured a silent prayer that he was doing the right thing. Frank only wanted the company, not Marcy. If given a piece of it, he might be content to leave Marcy alone.

"I'd like to propose that Annie be granted custody of Marcy, and that Frank Lester be named as a trustee, with Doc Adams, to control her share of the company until she is of age." Doc Adams would protect Marcy's interests, and maybe that was the best he could hope for.

In the silence that followed, all he could hear was the sound of Annie's indrawn breath and the beating of his own heart.

Annie tried to get her mind around Link's words, and she couldn't quite manage.

She thought several people started to speak at once, but all she clearly heard was the sound of crying. Marcy was crying.

Annie turned, half rising, to see the door to the judge's chambers open. Mrs. Bradshaw came in, carrying Marcy.

The woman murmured something that might have been an apology. She put the baby down.

"Nan!" Marcy toddled unerringly right into Annie's arms.

Annie lifted her, holding her close, murmuring softly. Link's arms were around the baby, too, his hand gentle on her back.

"Hush, sweetheart, it's all right." He stroked Marcy's blond curls. "Link and Nan are right here."

Marcy's tears vanished. She squirmed to a sitting position on Annie's lap, tilting her head back to give Link a ravishing smile.

"Here," she said proudly.

"Your Honor, this is unfair." The Lesters' attorney shot to her feet. "Mrs. Bradshaw's actions in bringing the child in could prejudice your decision."

"I'm sorry, Your Honor." Mrs. Bradshaw came forward, her eyes bright behind her glasses. "The baby started crying so hysterically that I felt I had to do something."

Judge Carstairs gave the social worker a long look. "That's strange, Enid. I've never known you not to be able to comfort a child."

Ms. Marshall was still standing. "Really, Judge Carstairs, you can't let yourself be influenced by the actions of a small child. I mean, naturally Marcy ran to the people who've been taking care of her for the past month. If my clients had more time with her—''

"That's enough, Ms. Marshall. I understand your position." She looked from one to the other of the people in front of her, as if she weighed each of them in the scales of justice.

Annie's heart seemed to stop as she watched the person who could wrest Marcy away from them. Link's hands were strong on hers, helping her hold the baby, but all the strength in the world wouldn't help if the court decided against them.

"Any custody case is difficult," Judge Carstairs said slowly. She tapped the tip of one polished nail against the folder on her desk. "A judge always feels like Solomon in a situation like this."

Link's hands tightened on hers, and his warmth flowed into her.

"I'm not making my decision based on the child's reactions, Ms. Marshall. I'm sure you'll be happy to hear that."

"Yes, Your Honor," the woman murmured.

"I'm making this decision based on the recommendation of the social worker and on my own observations. Luckily they happen to coincide." She rapped on her desk. "This is a very good vantage point. I can see everyone's face from here. When Mrs. Bradshaw brought Marcy into the room, I could see the love and concern on Mr. and Mrs. Morgan's faces. All they wanted to do was get to the child to comfort her."

She turned to level her gaze at Frank and Julia. "Unfortunately for your clients, Ms. Marshall, all I saw on their faces was annoyance at the interruption."

Ms. Marshall opened her mouth as if to protest, then closed it again.

"Like Solomon, I know that a child belongs with those who are willing to sacrifice for her." Judge Carstairs smiled. "Your particular sacrifice will not be necessary, Mr. Morgan. I'm granting unconditional custody of the minor child Marcy Conrad to Lincoln and Anne Morgan." She brought down her gavel. "That's all."

Through a haze of tears and happiness, Annie was aware of the congratulations and handshakes around her. All she could do was hold Marcy close. It was over. No one could take Marcy away from them.

The room cleared out quickly. Suddenly she realized that they were alone—Link, and Marcy, and her.

She looked at him with tear-wet eyes. "Link, I don't know what to say. You were willing to give away control of the company—" She stopped, choking on tears.

He took her hands in both of his, his gaze intent on her face. "I thought you might be mad at me all over again for making that decision without you."

"No. I understood what you were sacrificing. So did the judge."

"Annie, there's something I have to say, right now, before I lose my nerve." He brushed a tear from her cheek, his fingers very gentle. His eyes were wet with tears, too. "I thought I didn't know how to have a family. I'd pretty much decided that was never going to work for me. And then, all of a sudden, God gave me you and Marcy."

She nodded, unable to speak. God had brought good out of tragedy for her, too.

"I thought the company was the most important thing in my world—my ticket to acceptance." He gripped her hands, and his voice roughened. "Now I know how little that means in comparison to having you and Marcy in my life. If you weren't telling the truth about your feelings for me, you'd better say so now. Because otherwise, you and Marcy are going to be stuck with me forever."

She managed to smile through the tears that blurred her sight. Everything she'd longed for was being handed to her, just when she'd thought it was lost completely. Link had been in a corner of her heart for eight years. Now he occupied it entirely.

God had taken down all the barriers. He'd turned their sham wedding into a real marriage in His sight.

"I always tell the truth," she said, and she and Marcy went into his arms.

Epilogue

September had come again. Annie never saw September without a lingering sadness, even though the sharp pain of Becca and Davis's loss had muted after two years.

She sat on the deck of the new house, holding a mug of tea cupped in her hands, and looked across the lake. The hills had begun to show a hint of yellow and orange, a reminder that fall was here and winter not far behind.

After much discussion, she and Link had decided to move into one of the new homes Link had built on the lake—a home that they could make their own.

They'd rented the Conrad house to an older couple who doted on it. That house had been in Marcy's family for generations. She could decide what she wanted to do with it when she was old enough.

At the sound of voices Annie leaned forward, looking over the railing. Link and Marcy were walking up the path from the lake, back from their usual Saturday morning trip to feed the ducks. Link claimed those were the only ducks in the world that knew which day of the week it was.

She and Link were Mommy and Daddy to Marcy now. The change had come gradually, once Marcy entered nursery school and heard the other children talking about their mommies and daddies. It gave Annie a pang of sorrow from time to time, but she made sure Marcy didn't forget Becca and Davis, looking at their pictures and talking about them often.

"Mommy, we saw a million ducks." Marcy raced across the deck and pressed against Annie's knee. "Daddy says we'll have to take more bread next week."

"Maybe not a million." Link leaned over the back of Annie's chair and dropped a kiss on her forehead. "How's my girl?" He put his palms on her growing belly. "And how's my little boy?"

"Both grand. He's kicking up a storm."

"I want to feel baby brother, too." Marcy put her small hands next to Link's big ones. She erupted in giggles when the baby, seeming to know she was there, kicked hard against her palms.

Annie shared a smiling glance with Link, her heart overflowing with happiness. From the deepest of sorrows, God had brought them lives filled with more blessings than they could possibly count.

* * * * *

Dear Reader,

For a long time, I've wanted to write a story based on one of my favorite Scripture verses from the story of Samuel anointing young David. Probably the story spoke to me when I was a child because I was always the shortest one in class! It was reassuring to know that God didn't judge His children by other people's standards.

My grandson, Bjoern, helped me remember what children are like at twenty months, and many of Marcy's mannerisms are modeled on him.

I loved writing about Annie's quest to care for her sister's child. I hope you'll find a share of faith and encouragement in her story.

Please write to me at Steeple Hill Books, 233 Broadway, 10th Floor, New York, NY 10279, and I'll be happy to send you a signed bookplate or bookmark. Visit me on the Web at www.martaperry.com.

Blessings,

Marta Perry

AN ACCIDENTAL MOM

BY

LOREE LOUGH

Becoming Mrs. Max Sheridan was all Lily London had wanted, but he'd married another. Now Max is back—with his motherless son—and the dream is revived. But Max is afraid that Lily won't be prepared to take on a ready-made family. Can Max and Lily learn to trust in God's leadership… and in their love for each other?

Don't miss

AN ACCIDENTAL MOM

On sale October 2003

Available at your favorite retail outlet.

THE HARVEST

ALL GOOD GIFTS
BY
GAIL GAYMER MARTIN

AND

LOVING GRACE
BY
CYNTHIA RUTLEDGE

Counting your blessings?
Add two brand-new Thanksgiving stories,
which bring a message of love and faith
in one volume, from fan favorites
Gail Gaymer Martin and Cynthia Rutledge!

Don't miss
THE HARVEST
On sale October 2003

Available at your favorite retail outlet.

Love Inspired

BLESSINGS

BY

LOIS RICHER

She wasn't what he'd expected…but surgeon
Nicole Brandt is just the temporary assistant
Dr. Joshua Darling requires. The widowed dad
desperately needs help with his patients and his
three rambunctious daughters. But can Nicole make
him see she is his perfect partner in medicine—and
the perfect wife and mother for his family?

Don't miss

BLESSINGS

On sale October 2003

Available at your favorite retail outlet.